BROKEN:

bits and pieces of me

Glenda Thompson

Rattler Press

Contact information: glenda@rattlerpress.com

Rattler Press
PO Box 928
Charlotte, Tx 78011

Visit us at www.rattlerpress.com

Publishing History
Trade paperback ISBN: 978-1-963680-13-3
Digital ISBN: 978-1-963680-14-0

Published in the United States of America

DEDICATION

To Cregg

Without you, I would never have discovered
my voice. I'm so glad we tied a double knot in it.

LUMAS

BROKEN:

bits and pieces of me

Glenda Thompson

PREFACE

So much emphasis is placed on an author's voice. This collection of short stories and poems is my way of sharing with you how I developed mine.

Who am I?

I am a painter with words.

What's my story? I imagine it's a familiar story shared by many of us.

After a lifetime of listening to the negative voices in my head that say I'm not enough, I can't do it, and why bother, I stomped my foot down.

After slapping a piece of duct tape over her mouth, I buried old Negative Nancy in the hall closet beneath a stack of old winter coats and Grandma's quilts. Hey, I live in south Texas. We don't need the coats. A quick slam of the door and twist of the lock later and I was ready.

It was finally time to get those annoying people who would tap on the inside of my eyelids at night when I tried to sleep out of my head and onto the page where they could haunt others. I swear some nights I felt like Gulliver on the island of Lilliput, but the little people lived inside of me instead of on the outside. The constant chatter… oh my! Each begging to have their story told. Please, people, I need to sleep sometime.

Truthfully, my journey began many years before I vanquished Negative Nancy. Growing up in less than ideal conditions, I turned to books to escape the drunken screaming, yelling, and fighting. When I read, I escaped into worlds far different from my own. I could be a princess, an astronaut, a race car driver, a firefighter, or a woman madly in love in a world where love didn't hurt.

You get the picture. I wanted to provide that escape to others who might need it.

A sixth-generation Texan with Scottish roots, I can 'bless your heart' with the best of them. As a former emergency medical technician married to a south Texas lawman, I've used insider information from both our careers as inspiration to build my Broken universe of Texas Rangers with hidden pasts and dark secrets.

I also wanted to draw attention to subjects that often got swept under the rug and ignored. The heroes in my Broken series are all flawed. They screw up, hide secrets, and fail at solving their problems. You know, they're human.

My first novel, Broken Toys, addresses human trafficking and a Texas Ranger who isn't who he claims to be. Broken Dreams follows a different Texas Ranger—a single dad of three daughters—as he investigates a serial rapist who may or may not be a sheriff's deputy while fighting a growing opioid addiction of his own. I write gritty, compelling fiction with genuine emotion.

I also write snarky, fantasy romance for those days when my Broken world becomes too dark.

Many of the flash fiction pieces in this collection came from photographic prompts.

When I'm not huddled in my writing cave with Darlin', I can be found embarrassing my family by dancing in the middle of a country road during a rainstorm or enthusiastically ringing a cowbell to cheer on my grands at sporting events.

My advice for other writers? I'm going to steal a Jordan Bellfort quote: "The only thing standing between you and your goal is the bulls*it story you keep telling yourself as to why you can't achieve it."

Quit hugging the excuses. Put your butt in the chair, your fingers to the keyboard or pen to the paper, and write.

Or if you are not a writer, throw away all the bulls*it excuses you are hiding behind and chase your own dream. You can catch it.

Broken Toys

Words that itch burrow

Deep, deep, deeper into my brain.

"Who wants a broken toy?"

Crossing The Rio Grande

The faces of Illegal Immigration

The Mother

The plaintive cry of a coyote splits the night air in front of us. A second, behind us, answers. Shivers race down my sweat-soaked back. The weight of the backpack holding all my remaining worldly belongings — not that I have much left — digs deep into my stooped shoulders.

One weary hand clutches a gallon jug of water. The other clings to my most precious treasure, a whimpering child with a tiny backpack strapped to her back. Scratches cover our arms and legs from the brush; bruises from the men who brought us here.

I long to stop and comfort her but time is against us. Dawn lurks just over the horizon, a sullen vow to steal the protective shadows from the field and illuminate our flight. I tug her forward across the rocky ground, toward freedom, toward the American Dream.

Walk a mile in my shoes.

The Rancher

Sirens wake me. I glance at the clock. Three a.m.? I have to be up in an hour.

The familiar twang of breaking barbed wire and the shriek of crumpling metal force my feet to the floor. A bright light sweeps through my bedroom windows followed by the whomp-whomp-whomp of helicopter blades chopping through the air.

I throw on my boots and jeans, grab my shotgun, and step out on the front porch. A pickup truck trapped in the helicopter's spotlight careens crazily across the pasture coming to rest in a patch of brush. Hope they didn't hit any of my cows. So much for an easy day. Looks like I'll be rebuilding fence today. Third time this week.

Walk a mile in my shoes.

The Mule

Waves of queasiness pass over me. I taste rubber in the back of my throat. I hope one of the balloons in my belly doesn't break.

Packed in the backseat of this stolen truck with seven other men, fear battles with greed. I can smell my own fear. Success means more money than I have ever seen. Failure equals death.

Red and blue flashing lights flood through the back window. Terror cramps my stomach. Here we go.

Walk a mile in my shoes.

The Border Patrol Agent

I strap on my gear, adjust the weight of my Kevlar vest. Check my gun. Kiss my wife and children goodnight. Will I come home in the morning?

It's getting rougher out there. We're seeing fewer and fewer women and children, more and more young men with gang tats. A guy on my shift was jumped two nights ago. Six or seven illegals jumped him. Tried to bash his skull in with rocks. One stabbed him in the kidney. He's still in intensive care. Docs don't know if he'll make it.

I hold my family a little tighter before I head out the door.

Walk a mile in my shoes.

Holy Root Beer

(The Second Short Story I ever had published)

No serial killers, no cops, no blood or guts, but still a night that lurks in my memory forever.

Outside, dark clouds bruised the night sky. Wind whistled through the bare branches of the sycamore tree. Inside, the four of us wearing pigtails and flannel pajamas, huddled around a small, altar-like coffee table in front of a lace-covered picture window. Raindrops pelted the glass. The smell of vanilla, from thirteen flickering candles, filled the room.

"Okay, young ladies, keep it down to a dull roar and try not to set the house on fire."

A chorus of "yes, ma'ams" followed Grandma down the hallway to her bedroom. The click of her door closing cut off our only source of light save the candles scattered about the dining room.

With our hands held over our mouths to smother giggles, we crept to the kitchen. Carol and I took Grandma's rose-covered porcelain teapot out of the china cabinet.

Becky Anne climbed up and stood on the kitchen counter to remove the matching teacups from the top shelf of the cupboard.

"Careful," Tammy said as two cups clinked together, "Grandma will tan our hides if we break these."

One at a time, Becky handed the fragile, gold-rimmed cups to Tammy.

Carol poured lemonade into the teapot while Tammy and I placed four cups around the coffee table. "Okay," Becky whispered, "is everyone ready?"

Glancing at each other, trying to be serious and failing miserably, we all smothered smiles and nodded.

"Everyone sit on the floor around the table in a circle." Raising both hands above the teapot, Becky solemnly intoned, "Oh Great Spirits beyond the veil bless our holy lemonade."

"Holy lemonade?" I snickered, tossing a glance at my sister, Carol. Snorting through her nose, she burst into laughter.

"Glenda Kay! Carol Jo! Shhh. You're ruining everything. Get serious." Tammy scowled at us before turning to Becky. "Go on, Becky Anne, ignore the children." At the ripe old age of nine, Tammy loved lording it over those of us younger than she.

Glaring at me through her horn-rimmed glasses, Becky picked up the teapot and started again. "Oh Great Spirits beyond the veil, bless our holy lemonade." She filled each of our teacups. Raising our cups over the candle flickering in the center of the table, we gently clinked them together and drank. Becky passed the teapot to Tammy.

"Spirit of the East," Tammy refilled our cups, "Keeper of New Beginnings, we salute you." As one, we raised our cups to the eastern corner of the room, bowed and drank the cool, sweet lemonade. Tammy passed the teapot to me.

"Hey, the teapot's empty." I hopped up from my seat on the floor and headed into the kitchen. "Uh-oh, we're out of lemonade." Opening the refrigerator, I peered in. "What about holy root beer?"

Carol cracked up. She laughed until tears ran down her cheeks. I couldn't help myself. I joined her.

Becky shot to her feet and popped her hands on her hips. "Look, if you two don't want to do this, fine." She tossed her hair over her shoulder. "It's your baby brother we're trying to reach with this séance." She stormed from the room.

Carol followed her. "I'm sorry. It just sounded so funny — holy root beer. I'll try to be serious, okay? So will Glenda." She shot me a warning glance. "Please? Can we try again?"

Hot tears flooded my eyes, clouding my vision, at the thought of James Allen, the brother who never came home from the hospital. I poured the root beer into the teapot and walked back to the dining room. Things didn't seem so funny now. Subdued, I filled our cups. "Spirits of the West, Keepers of Dreams, we salute you." Turning to the west, we bowed and drank the icy root beer. I swallowed hard, forcing the bubbly drink past the pain blocking my throat. I handed the teapot to Carol who once again filled our cups.

"Everyone, look at the candle flame. Concentrate hard." Carol slipped into her 'spooky' voice. "James

Allen … James Allen … if you can hear us, send us a sign."

Lightning split the darkness as thunder roared through the night. A huge gust of wind rattled the picture window. Startled, we looked toward the window. Framed by the lace curtain a pale, ghostly face floated.

Screaming, we leapt up and raced down the hallway to Grandma's room. Carol ran into Becky who tripped over Tammy as we flew toward the doorway outlined in light.

Trembling beneath the quilt in Grandma's bed I wondered, did we really raise the spirit of our baby brother? Was it the neighborhood 'peeping tom' we had overheard our parents mention? Or was the face in the window merely a figment of four overactive imaginations on a sugar high?

Slipping silently from the room, I tiptoed back to the kitchen and filled a cup with root beer. Hands trembling, I placed it on the windowsill. Just in case James Allen wanted a sip of holy root beer.

Bad Sugar

Story prompt: Song Titles "Toys in the Attic"

"No!" I snatched the chocolate-covered, cream-filled eclair from his aged hands.

Thumping his cane against the floor, he grumbled, "Grown man... eat what I want..."

I flung my arms around him; kissed his balding head. "PawPaw, you heard Doc. I can't lose you like those old toys in the attic."

***

Uncontrolled Diabetes is a serious, sometimes life-threatening disease. Over time it can affect every body part and may cause kidney damage, nerve damage, amputations and blindness. It also raises your risks for heart and blood vessel disease and stroke.

Devil's Breath

Hot wind caresses my cheek. Sweat stings my eyes.

The crackling, rolling roar surrounds us, invites us to battle. The living, breathing entity devours all. We advance, pushing the demon back.

Bouncing, clinging to the tank, fighting the hose. Rushing water hits flames with a steaming hiss.

The battle continues.

Inside These Four Walls

Advice From Home

Two years ago, I was with my Grandma celebrating her 107th birthday. Six months later, she left this plane of existence for the next.

This year, on her birthday, I revisited her home that now sits empty, except for the ghosts.

Grandpa planted the magnificent Magnolia tree that shaded the house for decade upon decade for her when he finished building that home with his own two hands.

As I walked through the yard, I spent time thinking of all the things I learned within the four walls of this modest brick home. I wanted to share some of them with you.

EAT CAKE! Don't wait for the big things, celebrate life every day.

HELP SOMEONE NEAR YOU. Don't talk about it, just do it. Don't do it for the attention or the "attaboys", do it because someone needs help. Again, don't wait for the big things, like hurricanes, floods, or forest fires, help someone every day. Someone near you needs help now, even if it's just holding open a door or sharing your smile.

NEVER STOP LEARNING. Grandma believed if you let a day slip past without learning something new, you wasted that day. She also believed book learning wasn't the only learning available. Life isn't about learning how to take a test. Life is the test.

DREAM BIG and chase those dreams. You never know if you don't try. Some dreams are harder to catch than others so keep on chasing them. Who knows? You might catch your dreams right around the next corner.

LISTEN. Talk less, listen more. Actively listen—don't spend the time others are talking formulating your answers or next story. Stop and actually hear what others are saying. You might learn something.

HAVE FUN! Most importantly, live, love, laugh, and have fun. For as long as I can remember right up until the end, we teased Grandma about being a disco-dancing, black-leather-wearing motorcycle mama.

On her 99th birthday, she asked my Darlin' for a ride on his Harley. Life is short—or not. Take risks.

Everyone dies, but some never live. Treasure your family and friends. Embrace them and life with all you have.

I love you, Grandma, and I miss you. I miss your wisdom, your wicked sense of humor, and your sweet, sweet iced tea.

I love all y'all too, my family and friends.

PS: Grandma says "Don't you dare mess with that Magnolia tree."

Celtic Thunder

When the storm rages
Taranis hurls his stout wheel
forging a great din

He calls forth righteous
Fire from the air, its voice
Thunder following

Chameleon

I've seen your faces,
Many faces, hiding truth
Wicked chameleon

You change constantly
Never showing your true self
Wicked Chameleon

Hiding behind the
Words and actions of those
Surrounding you. Why?

Raindrops on Roses

Teardrops fall, gently
Caressing velvet petals.
Prepare. Change comes soon.

Red, White, and Blue

My biggest Fear

Red and blue lights race through the darkness. Red puddles pool on the pavement. Blue-tinged skin cools. Ambulance doors slam shut.

The gurney wheels clatter as it races through white halls. Doctors shout.

Bagpipes wail. Rifles fire.

White gloves hand me the red, white, and blue flag. Goodbye, my love.

Selling The Children

"That's it. I'm selling you to the gypsies."

"Buy one for the price of two, get one free," quipped my son, brushing the paint-soaked hair from his face.

His sister laughed and hit him with the paint gun, again... in my living room!

I stormed out of the house.

A week later, a knock sounds on the door disturbing my peace and quiet.

A gypsy. "How much to take them back?"

Querying

A Parallel Between Life and Writing

"Hey, Mom, can I borrow the keys to your truck to run to Brad's?"

Uh, no — aren't you like five?

I look up. A carbon copy of his father towers over me—strong and confident. *When did this happen? Did I create this?*

I look at my son, truly see him. Hope dances in his eyes. He's a good boy—really good.

With trembling fingers, I hand him my keys. "Call me when you get there."

A smile lights up his face. He zips off into the world.

I watch the clock. I pace the floor. *Silly, Mom, it takes time to get to Brad's.* Over and over again, I return to the window, eyes searching the road. I wait for the call.

Needing a distraction, I turn to my work in progress. I punch print. The printer whirs, spits out page after page after page. *Wait a minute. When did this happen? Did I create this?*

I sit and read. It's good—really good.

I type out a personalized query letter, and then another, and another. With trembling fingers, I hit send. My manuscript zips off into the world.

I pace the floor. I check my email. *Silly, Author, agents take time to respond.*

Clash

Confrontation of Seasons

Hair white like winter
Green eyes sparkle like springtime
Seasons clash within

Your Brains Were In My Hands—Literally

A remembrance of a volunteer emergency medical technician

Dear Soldier,

Your brains were in my hands—literally.

I did my best to hold them inside your skull where they belonged. I will never forget you. Why did you do this to me? When I close my eyes at night, I'm there with you again.

***

Heading to work at four in the morning, Darlin' is driving while I kick back in the passenger seat, feet propped up on the dash of my Mustang, trying to sneak in a few extra winks. We're cruising along I-10 at 80 mph, nice and easy on the open road.

A roar like a jet engine causes me to pop my seat upright. I see your truck wheeling past us at 100-plus miles per hour—end over end. What happened? How did you lose control? Did you fall asleep?

What used to be your truck but is now a crumpled ball of metal slides to a stop. Be grateful your truck went to the left and landed in the median. To the right is a steep, steep drop off into nothing but brush. That and my Mustang, with us in it.

We whip off the side of the interstate, parking on the shoulder. I race across two lanes of blacktop to reach you. "Darlin'," I yell, "grab my jump bag, please."

"Ambulance and DPS are en route."

Darlin' drops my bag at my feet and wrenches your door open.

Did I mention he's law enforcement? Thank God, he's six foot something and a wall of muscle. I would never have gotten the door open by myself. I kick away the pistol that falls out when the door opens and step in as close to you as I can get.

"Hey, Bud," I call you all Bud or Honey. I don't know your names, not yet at least. "Can you hear me? Help is on the way."

"Can you just take me home?" you ask.

"Where's home, Honey?" You name a town over four hours away—in the opposite direction. "That's a little out of the way, Sweetie. Hang in here with me, okay? Ambulance is coming."

I assess you for the A-B-C's. Airway-check. Breathing? Yep, you're talking to me. Circulation? Blood is definitely circulating. It's pouring from a wound on your head.

I sure hope you don't have anything contagious because I completely forgot to put my gloves on.

Quickly assessing your wounds in the dark is a challenge. You may have a broken bone or two, but the scariest thing is seeing your scalp peeled back and the bone open beneath it. Gray cheesy matter pulses in the opening. How are you even alive?

I keep talking to you. "Where are you going, Soldier?"

"How do you know I'm a soldier?"

I force out a chuckle. "Oh, I don't know. Tthe haircut, the pistol, and the BDUs might have given me a hint."

"Can you just take me home? Please?" Your words slur. Your eyes drift close.

"Come on, Honey. Stay with me. What's your name?" I check your carotid pulse. I can't reach your wrist. You are pinned beneath the steering wheel. I keep one hand pressed firmly against your head wound. Your brains are literally in my hands.

Your eyes flutter. They open. You make eye contact with me. "Can you please just take me home now?"

My heart clenches. My throat tightens. I'm afraid you may be going Home, not home. "It's okay, Hon, the ambulance is almost here."

There are more questions I should be asking. I try to take a medical history, check for drug allergies, ask what medications you might be taking. But every question I ask, you answer with a request to go home.

Darlin' shouts at me. "Get away from the truck."

Why would he say that? He knows I can't let go of you. I look up. A flicker catches my attention. Why not? What else could go wrong?

The flame in your engine compartment grows.

Darlin' yells again. "Get away. Now."

I yell back. "I can't abandon him. I won't."

He rushes to me, followed by a big burly bearded guy I've never seen before. The big guy is carrying a fire extinguisher. *Thank you, God!*

I can hear the sirens in the distance. "Hang on, Honey. Help's almost here."

Minutes pass feeling like hours. Your eyes drift closed again. I keep talking to you. Rambling on about anything and everything. The whole time I feel your warm blood slipping through my fingers, but you're a fighter.

You keep breathing. Keep asking me to take you home.

Finally, the professionals arrive. I give them a quick report. Vitals, mechanism of injury, observations. Turn your care over to them.

As I step out of the way, my calm vanishes. My legs buckle. Darlin' catches me. As the tears start to fall, I hear you ask, "Can you please just take me home?"

Coming Day

Free falling stars streak
Across the winter sky while
Flames dance in the dark

Crescent moon shines soft
Illuminating grazing
Deer on the hillside

Dancing Among the Stars

Mom, Mama, Mommy
Look at me, I'm flying now
My feet touch the stars

Please don't cry, Mommy
I can skip, and dance, and play
My pain's gone away

Gone Fishin'

The paper fairy vomited on my desk. Phone receiver pressed to my ear, three more lines ring, ignored by coworkers. Email chimes.

A customer in front of me. "I need…"

The boss interrupts. "Where's my…"

"I quit." I walk away.

Waves lap against the pier. I love this new life.

Grammar Lessons
Also known as the difference between my son and daughter

Pecking away on the keyboard, racing against the clock, trying to beat my latest deadline, I'm interrupted by a tap on my shoulder.

My teenage daughter, hair curled and make-up spot on, stands by my side. "Mom, me and Sandy are going to the mall."

I shake myself from the fog of my story and re-enter the real world. "Who?" I ask.

"Me and Sandy. There's a sale at that store we like."

"Who?" I raise an eyebrow and wait.

"Mom."

I wait.

Heavy sigh. "Fine. Sandy and I are going to the mall."

I smile. "Have fun, Sweetie."

I return to my story world. Clickety-clack, clickety-clack, my fingers fly across the keyboard. A knock on my office door interrupts. I sigh and look up.

My son stands in the doorway, decked out in camouflage, a rifle slung over his shoulder. His shaggy hair curls up beneath the edges of his cap. "Hey, Mom. Me and Brad are going hunting."

"Who?" I ask.

"Me and Brad."

"Who?" I raise an eyebrow and wait.

My son raises his own eyebrow. Looks me up and down. Stoops and peers beneath my desk.

He stands and asks, "Do your feet fit on a limb?"

Just In Time For Halloween

Thwack!

I jumped. My buttocks stung.

The imp, my grandson, scampered across the kitchen.

"Young man, you do not hit Grandma." I gave him my best glare. "If you do, she might turn into a witch."

Youngster didn't miss a beat. His face lit up. "Just in time for Halloween."

Cycle of Life

Petals fall. Blooms die.

Pain before celebration.

From death comes new life.

Dancing In His Arms

'Silver Wings' drifted
across the open air dance
floor. He held me close.

"Could you dance any
closer?" you hiss in my ear
tugging me away.

"Jealous much, Honey?
Where's your girl, Whats-her-name?"
I give you 'the look'

"Stop. I don't want her."
I look over my shoulder
at the man waiting.

"You were my first love
but HE is my forever
love. Our time is done."

*First loves make great memories. If you're lucky,
they make lasting memories.*
*In my case, not so much. First loves can turn
into jealous stalkers.*

The Mother's Curse

Aka Payback's A Bitch

Raising children can be challenging. You never know what might come out of their mouths or what they might do regardless of where they are or who is listening.

One day, I experienced one of those challenging days. I had driven my Grandmother to the grocery store for her weekly shopping trip. My four-year-old daughter accompanied us. She pitched a walleyed temper fit on aisle five because I told her no.

Finally, I told Miss Priss if she didn't straighten up and behave immediately, she was going to get a spanking.

Her bright blue eyes widened, and that lower lip trembled. She wailed, "I want my daddy."

I shook my head. "No, you don't. Your daddy would have already spanked you."

"No, he wouldn't." She tossed her waist-length, blonde hair over her shoulder, popped her hands on her hips, and looked me straight in the eye. "He thinks I'm too cute to spank."

Laughter erupted from aisles four, five, six, seven, and eight. I wanted to melt into the floor and disappear, but I couldn't. Instead, I had to help my grandmother up from that same floor where she was rolling around, laughing her head off.

I know the common phrase is 'laughing her ass off,'" but I also remember using the words 'Grandma' and 'ass' in the same sentence once before. I can still taste the soap.

After we returned home, I called my mom for support, guidance, and yes, to vent a little.

"Mom, you are not going to believe what your granddaughter did today."

"Hang on a minute," my mom said. I heard a thunk as the telephone receiver hit the top of her desk. A drawer opened, paper shuffled around, and a drawer shut. She picked up the phone. "Go ahead," she said, "what happened today?" So I told my mom what happened. I heard what sounded like a pen scratching against paper as she murmured supportive phrases.

Time passed. I had another child. The day came when I, once again, needed motherly advice. I called Mom. She answered, and I said, "Mom, you are not going to believe what your grandson pulled at school today."

Before I could say anything else, she interrupted me. "Hang on; I'll be right back." Once again I heard the receiver bounce against the surface of her desk. I heard drawers open, papers shuffling, drawers closing. Another drawer opened and more paper ruffling. Finally, she picked up the phone. "Okay, what did my precious grandson do?"

"Mom, I am so embarrassed. I got a telephone call from the principal. Seems my son and another little boy in his kindergarten class were standing on the sinks in the restroom aiming toward the drain in the middle of the floor. They were competing to see who could pee the farthest."

This time I didn't hear the pen scratch against the paper.

"Oh," she said in a voice filled with disappointment, "well, what are you going to do about that?"

Not really the response I was hoping to receive. And why did she sound so disappointed?

Again, time passed as it does. I stopped by my mom's house, and the kids went out in the yard to play. I started to tell her about another prank one of the children had pulled. She stopped me mid-sentence, rushed to her desk, opened a drawer and pulled out three file folders. She flipped open the one with my name on it. Inside the folder were several sheets of notebook paper. On each page was a list from top to bottom. Some of the lines had been crossed through. I noticed each of my sisters had a file as well. My youngest sister's folder was thicker than anyone else's.

My mom grabbed a pen and looked at me expectantly. "Well," she said, "who did what?"

"Mom, what's with the folders?"

"Oh, these?" She waved a hand casually over the folders. "These are where I keep my 'mother's curse' list."

"Mother's Curse list?" I asked. "What mother's curse?"

"You know," she said, "the mother's curse? The curse I placed on you and your sisters the day your firstborn child arrived. The curse saying may your child be as rotten as you were? All the horrible things you and your sisters did, all the mean little pranks you pulled, are recorded on these pages. Every time one of you calls to tattle on one of your children, I cross a comparable item off my list."

"Really?" I shook my head. "Really, Mom? All these times I've called you for help, you've been crossing things off a list?"

She just smiled.

From that day forward any time I called her to "tattle" as she put it, I would start the conversation with "Better grab your list."

The day my daughter and her friend shut down the school because of a lab "accident" in chemistry class, I heard the paper rattle and a pen scratch. How did my mom know my best friend and I had done the same thing?

Every time a child skipped school to go to the beach; or shot a deer on the way to school and brought it to Ag class to teach them how to skin and gut it; every time they snuck out of the house; every jump off of the cliff into the river during Senior class pictures; any and every little thing my children pulled, I blamed directly on my mom and her mother's curse.

Now my children have children. The other day my daughter called me.

"Mom, oh my God, Mom, you are not going to believe what Baby J did today."

I interrupted her. "Hold on, Sweetie," I said, "let me get my list."

Homemade Hooch

The rustic barrel
Contrasts with the smooth surface
Of liquid within

Silken warmth bubbles
Across my tongue. Tantalizes,
tickles my taste buds

The addition of
A rough seeded strawberry
Explodes the flavor

Textures mingle and
create a new masterpiece
Of sinful delight

Powder and Paint

Bottles and pots and jars and tubes littered the vanity. Round brushes, fan brushes, sponges—how was I to choose?

Metallics, mattes, a rainbow of options before me. A mask to hide behind.

But how was I ever going to learn how to use this paint for what I ain't?

The Devil's Daughter

Cobalt clouds bruise the sky
Seabirds hide, afraid to fly
Raging winds and roaring water
Here she comes, the Devil's daughter

Thunder crashes, lightning burns
Whirling, churning, currents turn
Rising tides race to slaughter
Here she comes, the Devil's daughter

Green-tinged skies, power vaster
Tornadoes spawned reap disaster
High winds pause, air grows hotter
Here she comes, the Devil's daughter

Silence falls, for peace we yearn
Strength builds, the storm returns
All the world is treading water
Here she comes, the Devil's daughter

Halfway there, we've passed the eye
How many souls will have to die?
Dark floods rise, buildings totter
There she goes, the Devil's daughter

On The Redus Trail

December 1863—Redus Stage Stop outside Devine, Texas

Sallie woke, cheeks wet with tears. "John?" She reached across the bed to the cool, empty place where her husband belonged. A sob caught in her throat. She stroked the rough cotton sheet. *Darling John, I miss you so.* She snuggled deeper beneath the covers. She ached to return to her dreams: dreams of the days before the death of their son, William; dreams of days spent together in laughter and love before the War and the Comanches forced her and her daughter to shelter in this two-room cabin with the others. Her emotions swung from one end of the pendulum to the next. *Fickle Fate, give him back. You've had him too long. Damn you, John. Why did you choose to leave us? Why did you choose war over me?*

She dashed the tears from her face. She knew how he would answer. He would say he chose war because of her; to keep her safe.

Oso, her black and white fur ball, poked his head out from under the blanket he shared with her. Head cocked, he sniffed the air. Laying his ears back, a low growl rumbled in his tiny throat. With a whine, he licked Sallie's nose.

She rolled over and burrowed deeper beneath the comforter.

Oso jumped on her shoulder, tapped her cheek with his paw. He jumped from the bed and raced across the hard-packed dirt floor to the front door. Barking furiously, he scratched at the oak and tried to dig under the door.

"Hush, Oso. You'll wake the children."

He scampered back to the bed, jumped up and began pawing at the blanket before grabbing it in his teeth and tugging on it.

"Okay, okay. You win. I'm getting up, but I swear if you wake Mary Jennette, I'm going to toss you outside to the coyotes." Sallie slipped a shawl around the shoulders of her flannel nightgown to ward off the chill of the December night before lighting a kerosene lamp. A sense of dread washed over her.

Her eyes darted to the bassinet of rough hewn cedar next to the kitchen table. Memories of finding William, still and blue, in that same cradle assaulted her. Sallie's breath caught. She raced barefoot to the crib. She exhaled with relief. Her daughter, Mary Jennette, slept peacefully. Placing the kerosene lamp on the table, she wrapped the patchwork quilt tighter around the child, tucking the edges around the toddler's chubby legs to guard against the cold.

Sallie yawned and looked out the window of the cabin, hoping to see John riding up the path. A rosy glow hinted at the glorious sunrise to come, but no John. *Damn this war.* A shiver ran down her spine. She glanced around the cabin. Nothing seemed out of place, but she could feel something was wrong.

Along the opposite wall of the cabin, her sister Annie and her two children huddled in their four-poster bed sound asleep. Tom, the ranch hand, lay on a pallet in front of the hearth, also sleeping. From the other room, she heard the rustle of a comforter and her father's raspy cough. Sallie returned to the window.

Outside, no night insects clicked or whirred. No frogs croaked or sang. The yipping coyotes who had kept her awake earlier in the night fell silent. *It's too quiet.* Fear filled her.

Oso circled at her feet, darting back and forth between Sallie and the door. His barking grew sharper and more frantic.

"Sallie, shut that damn dog up. People are trying to sleep here."

"Yes, Papa, right away." Sallie turned back to the dog. "Now you've done it, Oso. What is it, boy? What has you so upset?"

The dog scampered back to Sallie, hopping on his hind legs when he reached her. She bent down to scoop the black and white fur ball into her arms. A hissing, crackling noise reached her ears as the first hint of wood smoke tickled her nose. They had safely banked the fireplace fire. No sparks. She turned to the cast-iron stove sitting in the cabin's corner. Yes, it was lit, but the coals were smoldering—not flaming, not smoking—nothing out of control.

Shrill whinnies of fear split the silent night air. Oso trembled in her arms. Sallie dropped the dog on her bed and rushed back to the window and peered out. Her eyes widened. Her pulse quickened.

Brilliant orange and yellow flames shot through the roof of the barn. Inky black smoke billowed out around the shutters on the stall windows. The sound of hooves striking wood mixed with groaning timbers and screaming horses as fire consumed the dry wood structure.

"Papa—the horses! The barn's on fire." Sallie dashed to the door. As she struggled with the heavy crossbar securing it, a ropy black arm grabbed her around the waist and jerked her away. A short scream escaped her lips. Oso began barking again. The baby woke and began crying.

"Easy, Miss Sallie, easy. It's me, Tom."

Sallie clutched his arm. "Tom, thank the Lord. Help me save the horses."

He tightened his grip around her waist. "I cain't do that, Miss Sallie."

"Tom Sullivan, you unhand me this very instance. How dare you lay a hand on me? Let me go."

Annie sat up in the bed in the corner, rubbing sleep from her eyes. Her blonde hair escaped from its usually tidy braid and stuck out around her head like a porcupine's quills. She looked from Sallie to Tom. "What's happening?"

Tom released Sallie but placed himself between her and the door. Beads of sweat formed on his forehead. He licked his lips. Grim determination etched his dark features. In a low whisper, he repeated himself. "I cain't let you open that door, Miss Sallie."

Sallie shoved against Tom, trying in vain to move him. "Tom, step aside. Now. There's no time for this."

"What in tarnation is going on out there? Man can't even sleep in his own bed for all the racket. Shut that damn dog up. What's all the caterwauling?" The bed in the other room creaked as Papa climbed out of it. "Sallie, take care of that squalling kid of yours. Next thing you know, Annie's pack of brats will be up yammering at me, too."

"Papa, please. The horses are in the barn."

"Of course they are." Papa stepped into the main room of the cabin. He stretched and scratched his belly. "Where else would they be in the middle of the night?"

Sallie stomped her foot in frustration. "Papa, the barn's on fire."

"Well, what the hell are you standing here jawing for?"

"Mr. Daniel," Tom held out a restraining hand. "Don't open that door."

"Stop all this foolishness." Papa pushed his way toward the door. "If we don't get those horses out of that barn and quick, they're gonna burn to death. Now step aside, boy."

Annie's children awoke and added their whimpering to the baby's cries.

Tom's voice hardened. Tom's voice hardened. "You open that door and all of us, even them young 'uns, is gonna die a terrible hard death."

Sallie tried again to duck around Tom. "What nonsense are you spouting now? We don't have time for your haints and superstitions. Get out of my way." She shoved her shoulder against his chest. "Can't you hear them? The horses are dying."

"It ain't superstitions, Miss Sallie. It's Comanches. Them red devils done set that barn on fire to draw us out."

"I looked out the window. I didn't see anything."

"They're there. You may not see 'em, but they're out there. I can feel 'em in my bones." He pointed to Oso, who shivered beneath the blanket on the bed. "Even your little dog knows they are there."

As if on cue, an arrow shot through the open shutter, knocking over the lantern. Flames licked across the table, devouring the spilled kerosene, racing toward the crib.

"Mary!" Sallie cried as she and Annie raced toward the baby from opposite sides of the room. Sallie swept her daughter into her arms and flung her shawl at Annie.

Her sister beat the flames with the wool wrap, suffocating them before they could consume anything else.

Daniel and Tom slammed the shutters closed, locking them into place with a crossbar before rushing around the cabin, blocking off the rest of the windows.

Savage war whoops erupted across the night. Thundering horses' hooves vibrated the ground as the war party swarmed over the rise behind the barn. The Comanches raced past the burning barn into the yard.

Sallie kneeled in front of the closed shutter, peering out the rifle slit cut in it. Backlit by the flames, the full moon shining on their painted faces, the warriors presented a terrifying sight as they brandished their war lances and bows over their heads.

The chief shouted a war cry and waved his war hawk club toward the cabin. With a crazed roar, the braves surged forward.

She fell away from the rifle port, crumpling to the floor. She wrapped trembling arms around her stomach. Her mouth gaped open. She tried to speak, but no words emerged. Her pulse thrashed in her ears.

"Damn it, I knew we should have gone to Castroville with the others." Papa grabbed his Henry repeater and tossed it to Sallie. "Always make the wrong choices."

John wouldn't be able to find us in Castroville. I needed to wait here for him. An image of the wagon loaded with all their worldly belongings flashed through Sallie's mind. She saw it sitting at an awkward angle; the wooden spokes of the wheel shattered. "Not the way I remember it, Papa. You can't control everything."

He grabbed his Spencer, slapped a magazine in the breech, and worked the lever to chamber a round. "Annie, get those children gathered up and hide them in the wardrobe. Keep 'em quiet."

Tom rushed from the room, returning with another Henry rifle and a Greener shotgun. "Not like we really had a choice, Mr. Daniel. Stage kept running. We'd a job to do."

"Choice or not, we're paying for it now." Papa scrubbed a hand across his face. "Tom, hand that Greener to Annie and take the north rifle port." He barked orders. "Sallie, take the east port. I'll take the west. If it moves, shoot it, but don't waste no shot." A grim look passed from Papa's blue eyes to Tom's black ones. "If something happens to me and they break through…" Papa broke off and nodded toward the armoire. He swallowed audibly. Voice cracking, he said, "You know what to do. Save on for yourself, too."

"Papa, what are you saying? Papa? What…" Sallie's voice rose in pitch. Stories of women and children raped, disemboweled and burned alive by marauders whispered through her mind. Horror filled her eyes as understanding dawned. "Oh, Papa," she whispered, a hand clutching her throat. A hush fell inside the cabin, broken only by the muffled crying of the frightened children. Even Oso stopped his incessant barking.

She returned to her post in time to see a group of Comanches break off from the rest and charge the cabin on their painted war ponies. Others dropped to their bellies on the ground to slither snake-like to the cabin, shadows of death creeping through the dawn. Another bunch, whooping victoriously, guided the horses from the burning barn, driving them back toward the Comanche encampment.

Papa locked eyes with his oldest daughter. "Annie, use that candle and mold as much shot as you can, but if you hear movement on that south wall, grab that Greener and open fire." He turned to face Sallie. "You know what to do, yes?"

Sallie gave a sharp affirmative nod. Her hands shook as she lowered the trigger guard on her rifle and inserted the paper cartridges into the breech. Heart pounding in her throat, she glanced at the wardrobe. A pair of frightened green eyes met hers. "George Jr., shut that door this instant." Fear made her snap at her nephew. "Don't you dare open it again. No matter what. Do not open that door. Do you hear me? Keep that door closed and those babies quiet."

The door shut with a definitive click.

She peered out the eastern rifle port. The sight of the fierce raiders firing at the cabin caused her to tremble. The rifle slipped in her sweaty hands. Arrows thudded against the cabin walls. Their iron tips embedded in the thick adobe walls. Paralysis set in. Her heart beat wildly inside her chest like an eagle trying to escape the end of a tether.

Papa's voice jolted her from her trance. "Girl, whatcha' waitin' for? Get to shootin'."

Make every shot count. Leaning the rifle against the wall, she shook the tension from her hands. Squeezed her eyes closed. *Lord, guide my hand. Protect my family—wherever they may be.*

She picked up her rifle and aimed out the port. The stock of the Henry felt cool and smooth against her cheek. She focused her eyes down the length of the barrel. Holding her breath, she drew a bead on a brave and gently squeezed the trigger just like Papa'd taught her. As she exhaled, she saw the side of his head explode. In shock, Sallie's world went silent. Time ground to a halt. Blood, brain matter, and bits of bone flew outward from his temple in slow motion. His body flopped from his horse like a loosely jointed bag of bones. As it hit the ground, time returned to normal. Spooked, the horse reared, turned, and galloped away.

The cabin filled with gun smoke and the acrid smell of burned gunpowder. Rifle shots echoed within the confines of the cabin walls, mixing with the cries of the frightened children and Papa's expletives. "Damn it, where the hell do these red devils keep coming from?"

Wave after wave of Comanches swarmed across the rise behind the barn. For each one they shot, two rose and took his place. Arrows sang through the air.

Sallie fought to control her ragged breathing. She aimed at another invader. As she fired, he swung low on the side of his horse, disappearing behind its neck. Blood rushed through Sallie's ears. Her face grew hot. *Damn it, John. We need you.*

The warrior pulled himself back upright in the saddle. Guiding his horse in a circle, he whooped and taunted her. He shot another arrow at the cabin.

Sallie fired again. This time, the bullet plowed through his chest, a growing spread of crimson ran down his side. A look of surprise crossed his face as death clouded his eyes.

"Son-of-a-bitch." An arrow flew through the western rifle port and buried its tip in Papa's right shoulder.

Another slipped through the eastern port. Sallie felt the feather on the end of the shaft brush against her cheek. The stench of fear clogged her sinuses. Panic clawed at her throat. *We're all going to die.*

Annie grabbed a spare rifle, poured powder into it, grabbed a bullet, and rammed it into place. She fumbled the gun and accidentally discharged it. The shot slammed through the ceiling. A body fell from the roof. Something slammed against the side of the cabin. Tossing aside the empty rifle, Annie grabbed the Greener. She shoved the barrel through the rifle port and opened fire. From outside, a cry of pain echoed the blast of the shotgun.

A heavy thud landed on the roof, followed by another, and then another. Sallied looked up. A blade carved an opening in the ceiling. She gasped. "Papa, look." She pointed a trembling finger upwards.

Tom and Papa followed the direction of her hand. "Mr. Daniel, we're out of time," said Tom.

Sallie peered out her rifle port. A painted face leered back at her. She screamed. Pointing her rifle at the shutter, she pulled the trigger. The brave's face disintegrated in the muzzle flash.

Papa's shoulders sagged, the unbearable weight of his burden dragging him down. Another glance out the gun port straightened his spine with resolve.

He picked up his Army Colt. Flipping the cylinder open, he held the barrel up and poured powder into the chamber. His hands shook. Powder spilled onto the floor. He dropped in a ball and used the rammer to seat it. Sweat beaded on his forehead. Dampened the ends of his hair, sticking them to the back of his neck.

He repeated the process in each of the remaining five chambers before smearing grease over all six chambers to keep the pistol from chain firing. Turning the pistol over, he inserted a firing cap into each chamber. He pressed his quivering lips together. Grief filled his eyes as he resolutely turned toward the chifforobe.

"Papa, no!" Sallie dropped her rifle and raced to block the wardrobe door. Tears streamed down her cheeks. Her chest tightened, her heart heavy. "Please, Papa, please, no."

"Move aside, Daughter."

"No, Papa."

"Sallie, please." Papa's voice thickened with emotion, his expression strained. He dragged a quivering hand down his face. "Don't make this harder than it already is." He reached a hand out to shove Sallie from the front of the cupboard. "Do you know what these babies will suffer at the hand of those savages?"

Sallie's knees buckled. She collapsed to the floor and wept.

Papa pried the door open.

Sallie reached in and gathered Mary Jennette, holding the squirming child tight to her chest. George Jr. and Lisbeth peered out of the cupboard, their frightened, tear-stained faces pale in the darkness.

"Forgive me," Papa whispered. He raised the revolver. Blood from the arrow in his shoulder ran down his arm. He tried to thumb back the hammer on the revolver, but his hand was slick with blood and his thumb slipped. He grasped the pistol with both hands, using his left thumb to pull back the hammer. The cylinder of the revolver turned. His finger tightened on the trigger.

A rifle shot sounded outside the cabin. Sallie dropped Mary and lunged for Papa's arm, pushing down with all her might, forcing the gun to point at the ground just as the hammer fell on the firing cap. The round ricocheted harmlessly across the dirt floor. "Papa, wait. Listen."

More rifle shots interrupted the war cries of the Comanches. Sallie dragged Papa to the window. Together, they peered out the gun slit in the shutter.

Five riders, soldiers from the look of them, rode in from the north behind the war party, trapping the raiders between the burning barn and freedom. The battle turned away from the cabin.

One rider, clad in a tattered gray uniform, caught Sallie's eye. *There's something about the way he moves.* As she watched him, the rest of the battle faded from her awareness.

He rode out ahead of the others. The Comanche chief answered his challenge, riding out to meet him, firing his bow.

The rider ducked. The arrow zipped past him.

The chief released two more arrows in quick succession.

The soldier turned his horse, and both arrows missed. Spurring his stallion into a run, the soldier charged the chief, firing his pistol.

The chief swung down to avoid the bullets, clung to the side of his pony, and returned the charge. Upon meeting the soldier, he pulled himself upright and swung his war hawk, hitting the soldier's hand.

The soldier's pistol clattered to the stones on the ground. As they wheeled and ran at each other again, the soldier drew his saber from its scabbard. He blocked the war hawk with his sword.

With a cry of anger, the chief jumped the soldier, knocking him from the saddle.

Sallie stared helplessly, one hand clutching her throat, the other wrapped around her stomach, fighting nausea. She knew if this soldier died, her family was next.

The men struggled to their feet. Using a scalping knife, the Comanche struck at the soldier. The soldier blocked the strike with his left arm while pulling a Bowie-type knife from the sheath at his waist. They circled one another warily, feinting and thrusting, testing for weaknesses. The soldier lunged at the chief. His knife sliced the warrior's arm, drawing first blood.

The chief grabbed the soldier by the wrist, pulled him close, and slammed an elbow into his face.

Reeling back, blood gushing from his nose, the soldier shook his head, trying to regain his bearings.

On foot, the chief surged forward, throwing the soldier to the ground. As they hit the earth, the soldier tucked and rolled, ending up on top of the warrior.

Sallie held her breath.

Over and over they rolled, each struggling to stay alive, to dominate, to win. They rolled until they smashed into the burning barn. Sparks showered down on them as they hit the collapsing structure.

The chief pinned his opponent to the ground.

Sallie gasped in horror as the chief, silhouetted against the flames, raised his knife. With a victorious cry, he plunged the blade down toward the soldier's chest.

A loud report echoed inside the cabin. A mist of blood filled the air in front of the barn. The chief collapsed in a heap on top of the unmoving soldier. Tom reloaded his rifle. "Sorry, I couldn't do that sooner. Didn't have a clear shot."

Seeing their leader fall, the other warriors paused in shock. More gunshots than war whoops echoed across the pasture as the soldier's companions took charge of the fight, turning it into a rout. The remaining braves leaped to their horses, some riding double to escape.

Sallie rushed to Mary Jennette and scooped her up, wrapping the screaming child in her arms, holding her tightly against her chest. She turned to Papa.

He shook, his complexion gone ashen. "My God. The children…" The pistol fell from his hand. "I almost…"

"But you didn't, Papa, you didn't." Still clinging tightly to her daughter, Sallie led the weeping man to a rocking chair and helped him sit. "Here." She handed Mary to Papa. Kneeling at his feet, she patted his hand. "Lady Fate stepped in."

She turned and looked up at Tom. "Thank you."

Tom merely nodded. He threw open the shutters and watched as outside, the soldiers regrouped. The one who had battled the war chief staggered to his feet and gathered his weapons from the ground. He rounded up his horse, mounted, and rode fast for the cabin.

Tom opened the door as the rider reached the front door.

Sallie stepped to the doorway. Motioned to Papa to hand Mary Jennette to her.

Covered in dust and drying blood, shaggy hair and full beard covering his gaunt face, the rider slid from his horse and dropped to one knee, words of prayer tumbling from his lips.

She stepped onto the porch, Mary Jennette pressed tight to her chest. She crossed the yard until she towered over her family's savior.

The gray-clad soldier looked up, meeting her eyes, drawing her to him with his gaze.

Falling to her knees, she stood Mary on her wobbly toddler legs in front of her. Tears streamed down her cheeks, and she said, "John, meet your daughter."

Yin and Yang of Love

Which is easier
To love or to receive love
Which brings the most joy

Receiving the love
Of a pure shining spirit
Filling you with warmth

Or pouring your love
Into a warm, willing soul
Watching while it grows

Which bring the most pain
Being loved by a mad man
Possessed and controlled

Or to hold, shelter
Give all to another heart
Just to see it stop

End of Watch
Twenty years later, we remember
the Atascosa County Massacre

Twenty years have passed.

The wail of bagpipes still stops my heart.

Pageantry and pain.

My throat clogs with tears.

The flag faded.

My love has not.

Hurricane

Arguing with a Centenarian

Wind rips trees from earth
"Grandma, I'm coming for you."
"No, ma'am, you are not."

Sympathy for the Devil

Prompt: Song

Michael stretched his legs out toward the fire as he settled into the leather armchair, rattling the ice in his whiskey glass. His shoulders popped as he wiggled his snowy-white wings.

"Really, Lucy? Sympathy? You? The only place you're gonna find sympathy is the dictionary. It's somewhere between shit and syphilis." He laughed.

Lucifer's eyes flashed in anger. "Sanctimonious angels."

Wild Things

Seeking wild places
Deep within my tortured mind
Find the path to light

Wait For Me

Heart crumbles to dust
You slip silently away
Wait for me, My Love

Going Under

Tonight I'm drowning
Pulled beneath the surface by
The sins of my soul

I reach for my glass
Empty — I grab the bottle
Who needs a glass?

Fiery liquid burns
The back of my throat and my
Stomach deep inside

Still not enough fire
To burn away my dark sins
Tonight I'm drowning

Those Who Die With the Most Toys

Growing up, I loved spending time with my grandparents. Summer was magical.

PawPaw was a whiz with his hands. He taught me to measure twice and cut once. A big man, he was as gentle as they came.

He could fix anything. Bike chain popped off? No problem. Lawn mower won't start? No problem, he could handle that.

Best part about taking a problem to PawPaw? He didn't solve it for you. He guided you into realizing what was wrong and showed you how to fix it yourself.

Geen knew everything about wildlife. She hatched turkey eggs in her oven, took care of Canadian geese, and bottle-raised a squirrel.

We would walk the creek banks with her in the early morning, shoes soaking up the dew that coated the grass and made the sand glisten in the pre-dawn glow. We carried plaster-of-paris kits and searched for raccoon or other animal tracks to make casts of.

And cookies. We made the best cookies in her kitchen when she wasn't teaching us how to make bread from scratch.

I still enjoy kneading bread dough. Releasing that yeasty scent transports me back to her kitchen every time. Who said time travel was impossible?

And then there was Grandma. She didn't help us fix things. I never remember baking with her, and yet… she was Grandma.

When my first grandchild was born, all the grandparents were picking their grandparent names. Each of them wanted something different, a unique name no one else in the family had. Our grandkids have a Tutu, a Poppy, and a Nonni.

I asked my grandchildren to call me Grandma in honor of my grandmother. She was my safe harbor in the storm of life. I learned so many life lessons from Grandma.

One of my favorite sayings of hers was "Those who die with the most toys are still dead."

Now I know she wasn't the only person, or even the first person, to say this. But she was my favorite.

When she said this to me, I was working two jobs and struggling to raise two young children on my own.

Life was determined to bury me alive. I never had enough sleep. Some days, I wasn't sure I could even breathe.

One day, we were visiting her house. The kids were being active, healthy kids, but I was tired and cranky. I snapped at one of them for something inconsequential, something that normally I would have laughed off.

Grandma didn't raise her voice. Didn't give me one of those I-know-you-can-do-better looks. In no way did she indicate she was disappointed in me, although I thought for sure she was. She didn't warn me she was about to change my life forever.

She just glanced up at me. Gave me one of her Mona Lisa smiles and said, "Those who die with the most toys are still dead."

With those ten words, she stopped me in my tracks. Think about it. Those who die with the most toys are still dead.

No way around it. None of us are getting out of this life alive.

So why not focus less on accumulating material things and spend that energy making memories, sharing laughter, and creating new stories with those you love?

Until next time, remember what Grandma said.

A Day in the Life

Working in the office of an oilfield supply company

The paper fairy
regurgitated on my
heavy metal desk

The putrid odor
of sour gas wafts off the
clothing of the hands

Metal grinds, sparks fly
off tubing anchor catchers
and old downhole pumps

Grandgirl visits me
at the office. She's two.
PawPaw comes with her.

She sits at my desk.
Sour gas follows a hand in.
She frowns. "PawPaw fart."

In the Back of Her Head

Prompt: Eyes

"Stop picking on him.

You know I can see through walls."

Mom's eyes spy it all…

Way Back When

A Picture is Worth A Thousand Memories

I blink against the sudden flash.

Laughter drifts on a sultry breeze. The same breeze tousles my hair, caresses my cheek. The sweet, fizzy taste of soda tickles my tongue. The sun stings my reddened shoulders. Coconut and saltwater tease my nose.

Deep sigh. I snap the photo album closed.

The Lottery

A historic haiku

White beans mix with black
Drum rolls, blindfolds, rifles crack
Blood pools at my feet

Under the Big Top

Obscurity brushes over the King

as easily as it does the donkey,

sparing the clown of the famed circus ring

and elephant dancing with lustful glee.

Chasing fame becomes a laughable goal,

an essential race to reach the mirage,

A race taking a heavy, heavy toll,

Ending with a killing in the garage.

Adding powder and paint for what he ain't,

Life leaves him behind as he chases fame.

Poor King, on his knees, needs a patron saint

to help him salvage the end of the game.

"Too late," cries the Donkey. "Too late," the clown

Still the elephant dances around town

Hope Springs Eternal

"Hey, Cutie." A wink accompanied the words. "Wanna play?"

She looked at him as he leaned against the pool table, a halo of blue-lit cigarette smoke surrounding his head. "Who me?"

He rolled his stick between his hands, bouncing it, pointing it at her. "Yeah, you." He wiggled his eyebrows.

She rolled her eyes, shook her head. As she walked away she heard him say, "Hey, Cutie. Wanna play?"

I Failed

If you never know failure, you will never know success. —Sugar Ray Leonard

I hear you, Sugar Ray, I hear you, and if you are telling the truth, I will be the biggest success ever. Because I keep failing.

I promised myself I would post something on Medium, a publishing platform, multiple times a week, every week.

Um, yeah, that hasn't happened yet. I have a ton of excuses but I won't waste your time. Let's just say I failed—again.

I promised myself I would send out my newsletter this week, and once a week from now on. Did you get a copy of my newsletter? Yeah, neither did anyone else. I failed. Again.

I told myself I would have the third novel in the Broken Badges series finished by now. You know what's coming, right? Yep, you guessed it. I failed.

How do you deal with failure? Do you let it beat you about the head and shoulders until you curl into a fetal position and give up on everything? Do you let it tell you what a waste of human flesh you are?

No? Just me? Okay, then.

Clean slate time. I'm going to figure out this failure thing and overcome it.

Research teaches me the first thing I need to do is place the failure in proper perspective.

Sure, I didn't do things I promised myself I would do, but I didn't kill anyone, did I?

I took care of my family, completed the duties of my day job, and kept my pets alive. That counts for something, right?

I'm not going to beat myself up. Well, not too much. We need to learn to speak to ourselves the way we would talk to a dear friend, or a stranger.

Isn't it weird that often we are nicer to strangers than we are to ourselves?

I'm going to be grateful for the things I did accomplish. I wrote a few more chapters in my next novel. I created new pieces of fused glass. I survived another week. That's good, isn't it?

I am going to acknowledge my weakness. Lord knows I couldn't organize my way out of a wet paper sack.

At the same time, I am going to acknowledge my strengths. I may not be conventional but I am a cheerleader to those around me, and I think outside of the box. What are your strengths?

Last, I'm going to set a new plan for the next week.

I'm going to set reasonable, measurable, achievable goals and develop a plan on how to reach them. I'm going to break that plan into daily to-do lists and I'm going to work hard crossing things off each list.

What I'm not going to do is give up. What about you? How do you deal with failure?

Who?

Ever wonder who
I was before I was you?
Why here and why now?

Who were you before
You were me? Who were we then?
Who are we today?

War and Peace

Can peace exist in
A world that does not know war?
Would it be taken
For granted with nothing to
Threaten to take it away?

Two sides of the coin —
Would our perspective change if
Only one remains?
Would tranquility become
A worthless state of being?

It has been said that
There can be no sunshine if
There is no rainstorm.
Can there be true harmony
In a world that knows no strife?

It's Time

Prompt: Country Song

"It's done, ya'll." I drop the shovel.

Hair sticking to my neck, I wipe my face, smearing dirt everywhere. Sweat pools on my jean's waistband. Blisters burn my palms.

I chug a glass of ice-cold sweet tea, quenching my thirst. Rolling the glass across my forehead, I ask my sisters. "We ready?"

We all agree.

Earl has to die.

Dawn

Realization
Fills her eyes with hopeful light
New knowledge dawns bright

The Ride

A Cowboy Short Story

The odor of bulls, sweat, and fresh-manure
floated above the arena. AC/DC's "Highway to Hell"
thundered from the speakers, vibrating through
Rhyden Parker's chest. His bull rider's vest squeezed
against his ribs. He scanned the crowd sitting on the
wooden bleachers outside the welded pipe arena. She
wasn't there.

As he readied himself to ride, the music's
volume dipped and the rodeo announcer began his
spiel.

"Now, Ladies and Gentlemen, turn your
attention to chute number three. The cowboy inside is
a local boy, Rhyden Lupan Parker. That's right.
Rhyden "Wolf" Parker is a genu-i-ne descendant of
Comanche Chief Quanah Parker. Harper, Texas is
where he checks his mail. For tonight's short
go-round, he drew one of the rankest bulls in our

circuit — Voodoo Child. No muley this one; the horns on that bull can gut you faster than a hot knife through butter."

Rhyden tugged his riding glove a bit more snuggly on to his right hand. He threw a leg over the bull's back and wrapped the bull rope a little tighter around his hand. He lifted himself up, pulling on the chute gate, then settled firmly on the back of Voodoo Child. His mind drifted to the last conversation he had had with Cara. *Could she be right? Did he have a death wish?*

The bull bucked, slamming against the constraints of the chute. He pinned Rhyden's leg against the far wall.

"Hey, man, you okay? You seem a bit distracted." The flank man slapped Voodoo Child sharply on the hindquarters. The bull released Rhyden's leg.

"I'm okay." Rhyden pulled his attention back to the here and now. He eased back down onto the bull's back. He threw his chaps up over the tops of his thighs so they wouldn't become tangled around his legs and pull him off balance. Scooting closer to his riding hand, he pressed his Stetson firmly on his head with his free hand. With a sharp nod, Rhyden signaled the gate man.

The gate man pulled on his rope and scrambled up the side of the arena fence to get out of the way. The chute flew open. The beast surged forward, twisting and jumping.

"Here he goes! Come on folks! Let's help this cowboy out. The more noise you make, the easier it is for these cowboys to stick to the back of those bulls. Watch out there, cowboy, he's spinning away from your hand." The rodeo announcer continued working the crowd.

Why do they bother? Rhyden thought as the noise of the crowd and the announcer faded away. His entire world wrapped around himself and the 2,000 pound pissed off animal trying to throw him from its back.

Rhyden fought to keep his balance. *Eight seconds. That's all I need.* Using his free hand as a counterweight, he forced his body to stay loose. Adrenaline flooded his system, speeding his heart rate and tightening his muscles. *Stay loose. Don't think. Six more seconds.*

As the Brangus bull spun back to the right, into his hand, Rhyden felt himself being pulled into the well. Not a good place to be. *Hold it, hold it. Three more seconds. You've got this.*

Without warning, Voodoo Child whipped back to the left and jumped straight up. He landed with all four hooves slamming into the arena dirt. The jolt jarred Rhyden's spine and threatened to unseat him. The smell of burning rosin filled the air. The battle between beast and man continued.

The buzzer sounded, pulling Rhyden back to his surroundings. The cheering crowd noise surrounded him, pounding at him. Reaching down, he loosened the bull rope and jumped from the back of the bull without waiting for the pickup man. Stepping out of the still snorting, still kicking bull's path, he watched the bullfighters in their clown finery chase Voodoo Child from the arena.

"And that, boys and girls, is how it's done." The rodeo announcer continued, "Not many can cover a bull like our Rhyden Parker. Hold up a minute, folks. The judges are tallying their scores. Half the score comes from the cowboy. The other fifty points come from the bull. I think it's fair to say Voodoo Child did his job. Let's see what the judges have to say."

He paused as one of the three judges passed him a slip of paper. "Rhyden Parker scores a ninety-five, folks. That will definitely put him in the money. Let's hear it for the cowboy."

The crowd exploded in applause. Rhyden bent down, scooped his battered black hat from the dirt floor of the arena and waved it at the crowd. He beat the shabby Stetson against his leather chaps before jamming it back on his head.

Scanning the bleachers again, he tugged off his riding gloves. Not finding what he was looking for, he headed over to the back pens to grab his gear. He ignored the jolts of pain shooting through his hips and knees as he limped from the arena.

Spying Cara standing at the edge of the dusty, gravel parking lot bordering the arena, Rhyden threw his vest and rope over his shoulder and loped toward her. He felt a smile lift his cheeks.

Her long, slim legs were encased in high-waisted black jeans. With her sorrel hair slicked back into a French braid, she looked younger than her forty-two years, much younger.

Rhyden slowed and felt his smile fade as his gaze took in the suitcase at her feet. The darkness welled up inside him. For just a moment, a deep, helpless pain crushed his heart only to be stashed deep beneath his calm, icy demeanor.

Cara reached out to caress his cheek. With anger hiding hurt, he jerked away from her. Her hand fell limply to her side. Sorrow filled her eyes.

"Nice ride," she said.

"So," Rhyden rocked back on the worn heels of his scuffed riding boots. "You're really leaving." He stuffed his hands into the back pockets of his Wranglers to avoid reaching for Cara.

She took a step back, shrugged and crossed her arms over her chest. A question in her eyes, she looked up at Rhyden. Hope entered her voice. "I guess that's up to you now, isn't it?"

He remained silent.

"Well?" Cara bit her bottom lip. Her eyes glistened with unshed tears. Still no response from Rhyden. He kept his emotions tamped down, not allowing anything to show.

"Do you want me to stay?" Desperation punctuated each word. Cara swallowed hard. "Are you willing to get help?"

Why won't you let this go? Don't you know I love you, Cara, like no one I have ever loved? The thoughts crashed through his brain, but no words crossed his lips. He simply stared at Cara and waited. Waited for her to abandon him like so many others before her.

"Damn you." She pounded her fist against his chest. "You still won't let me in, will you? You can't do this on your own. You know that. You've spent your whole life bottling things up. Are you even capable of feeling anymore?" She muffled a sob. "I can't. I can't do this anymore. I'm done. I'm too tired. I can't keep fighting. You win. I'm gone." She picked up her suitcase and turned to walk away.

Rhyden reached out to her, snagged her around the waist and turned her to face him.

"What do you want from me? You want me to 'share'?"

He sneered. "What don't you get? My former line of work wasn't exactly dinner table conversation. You want me to tell you about the grocer down the road who got his brains blown into the watermelon bin by a two-bit meth addict? You want all the gory details?"

He paused. "Pass the peas, honey," he continued in a voice laden with sarcasm. "By the way, remember that other detective, my partner, you know—the one who brought his wife and kids over for dinner the other night? Yeah, well, he bled out in my arms. His hot blood pulsed out of a gunshot wound in his chest, covered my hands and arms up to the elbows. Each beat of his heart pushed him closer to inevitable death. He died, right there, with me covered in his blood and vomit. Oh yeah, I was the one that shot him. Hey, pass the catsup, would ya'?"

Rhyden's voice trailed off. He swallowed down the lump in his throat. "Is that what you wanted to hear? Is that what you wanted me to 'share'?"

He pushed her away in disgust.

Tears slipped from Cara's eyes. "Grow up, Rhy. You know that's not what I'm saying." She stepped away from him. "You have to let the past go before it completely destroys you. I know what happened. Edwards made a choice. I'm sure you did what you had to do to survive."

Darkness rose up stronger inside Rhyden. "What do you mean you know what happened?"

Startled by his menacing tone, Cara took another step away from Rhyden. "I know, okay? I know you shot Edwards. I just don't know why, and it scares me."

With the speed of a rattlesnake strike, Rhyden grabbed her arm and jerked her close to him. "Who told you that? You don't know what you are talking about." He gave her a violent shake. "Who have you told? You can never tell a single soul what you just said." He shook her again, harder. "Do you hear me?"

"You're hurting me, Rhyden. Let go." Cara jerked away from his grasp and stepped away rubbing her arms.

The darkness receded. He saw the red marks he left on her arms. Humiliation and rage at himself flooded through Rhyden. "Cara, baby, look. I'm sorry." He reached to take her in his embrace.

Cara moved further from his reach. "I'm sorry, too, Rhy. Really sorry. I love you, more than you will ever understand or let yourself accept, but I can't live like this anymore." She wiped tears from her cheeks, inhaled deeply, and squared her shoulders. "I'm going to stay at Kim's. You have my number. When, and if, you figure out how to be a whole person, how to have a real relationship, call me. But don't call me until you've gotten some professional help. I mean it, Rhy. Don't call." She grabbed the handle of her luggage and walked away.

Rhyden slumped in defeat. The opening bars of "Silver Wings" drifted across the parking lot as the band cranked up on the open air dance floor on the other side of the arena. Pride struggled with need as he watched Cara drag her suitcase through the gravel. *Go after her, you idiot.*

Rhyden started after her but the darkness rose again and shut him down.

Tilling the Field

rusty old tractor
turning the fertile red dirt
life's ancient cycle
of death, rebirth, and new life
repeats time and time again

It's Up to You

Life's all about choice
Happiness — a decision
Lonesome ends in me

Journalism

Who what where when why
The basic tenements of
Searching for the truth

Life's Journey

Prompt: Beginnings and Endings

"Hello?"

She twirls the phone cord around her fingers. "Tomorrow? Sure."

***

Wedding bells ring.

"Hello, wife."

She blushes, grins. "Hello, husband."

***

He rests his head against her blonde one in the hospital bed.

Together they whisper, "Hello, Son."

***

Beeping fills another hospital room. Becomes one persistent tone.

Tears fall.

"Goodbye."

Desk Job

"Don't worry. It's a desk job," he reassured me.

Memories of bloody bandages danced in my head. I wasn't reassured. Thoughts of bagpipes playing Amazing Grace haunted my dreams.

Days passed. I relaxed. Too soon. My phone rang.

"Hey, Sweetie, if I don't answer, don't worry. We're doing a drug raid. I'm kicking in the door."

Silence.

"Sweetie, are you there?" he asked.

"I hope you're taking your desk."

The First Time

A Young Man's Journey

Guilty desire smoldered in his eyes as he snuck into the darkened garage.

Does his father know he's here?

With trembling fingers, he caressed my curves, admiring, worshiping.

So young. Not a day over sixteen I'd wager.

He grew bolder, opening me carefully, slipping into my buttery warmth. He plunged his stiff key into me.

I purred to life, all eight cylinders, prepared to give him the ride of his dreams.

On the Banks of Hondo Creek

I carry my kayak to the river's edge. Which way to go?

Most would ride the current downstream where laughter and music beckon.

Silently, I slid my kayak into the cool, green water. I turn and steer against the current, fighting against nature, much as I have my entire life.

Once Upon a Time

The steady thump of pirate drums moving closer makes the hair stand up on the back of my neck. Darkness inches closer coming from the corner of the room. The skeleton hanging from a silver rack behind the old leather wingchair rattles.

A frisson of fear races down my spine.

It's only a story.

The pirate drum beats faster, louder. The sweet scent of roses drifts through the room.

I slam the book closed and hide.

Passage to Hope

When the dark of night

Creeps in, surrounds and threatens,

Hold tight, dawn soon comes

Through the Wife's Eyes

He protects and serves
Every day I say goodbye
Will he come home safe?

The star on his chest
Used to make him a hero
Now it's a target

I sit and worry
Lights flash across door. He's home.
I can breathe again

The Nursery

A Haiku Series about Endometriosis

Pain and cramps and tears
Won't you make it go away?
I'm too old for this

Take out the nursery
Put in a playroom I plead
But doctors say nay

I double over
Pain crippling me, killing me
Stabbing deep inside

Frivolous they say
Suck it up, Buttercup
And they walk away

Perspective

Through Their Eyes

Look in the mirror
I hate those gray strands until…
"Grandma, you sparkle."

Southern Blessings

"Well, bless your little heart."
Innocent words tinged with hate…
Why did we twist it?

Proposition?

The band blasts country music in the corner. Smoky air wreathes the patrons. The sharp scent of whisky mixes with the warm smell of beer.

The song ends. The band begins counting down to the new year. "Five - four - three…"

Warm breath brushes my ear. "Guess where I want to be by the end of next year."

I shrug. "Out of debt?"

"Reach into my pocket."

Slap! "Pervert."

"Seriously."

Tentatively, I reach into his front blue jean pocket. His grandmother's wedding band rests there. I giggle.

"Is that a yes?"

"Is that a proposal?"

Crowds surge tighter around me, lifting toasts and kissing. I succumb to an uncontrollable fit of giggles and there you go.

***

Darlin' proposed in the exact same corner of the bar where we met. Twenty-five years later, I

still love him. More importantly, I still LIKE him…
a lot… and he still makes me giggle
uncontrollably.

So much so that we tied a double knot in it on
the beach after twenty-three years of marriage.

Rainbow Chasing

Tanka Prompt: Dawn

Birth of a new day

Bringing promises of hope

And threats of sorrow

Make wise choices and follow

Your dreams into the sunset

Shattered

The Day Time Stood Still

"Mom, don't freak out." My daughter-in-law kept talking.

The phone fell from nerveless fingers. My heart stutter-stepped. Why do they always start bad calls with those words?

Scary images raced through my mind. She texted the photos. My imagination had nothing on reality.

I beat the helicopter to the hospital.

— — — — —

For those who are wondering, my son survived and is doing wonderfully. He has a fancy-schmancy titanium rod embedded in his femur. When he woke up after the three hour surgery that lasted six hours, the first thing he told me was "God was riding shotgun."

The wreck occurred when he was on his way to work on an oil rig in South Texas. An oncoming vehicle blew a tire, lost control, crossed the line and hit him head on. The other driver walked away without a scratch.

Please keep your vehicles in good condition.

When we showed him photos of his truck, he said, "Maybe I should stay home and build dog boxes for a living."

Ripples on a Pond

Drift on the surface
Smooth as glass until the wind
Wrinkles the calm pond

Undulating waves
Create a forward movement
Reaching for the bank

Still drifting along
Spinning against the current
Riding out the storm

SHHHH—

Haiku Prompt: Quiet

A hush engulfs our
home. No more tears, no more joy,
The nest is empty.

Taking Back

Haiku Prompt: Begin

The virus set free
Unleashed on unsuspecting
Civilizations

Ivy creeps forward
Mother Nature surrounds man-
Made items. Reclaimed

Humanity goes
The way of the dinosaurs
Mother Nature heals

The world starts again
Slightly scarred, slightly worn
But fresh. Clean, new start

Texas Tea

Pounding, burrowing,
Puncturing deep, Mother Earth
Searching for black gold

The Folded Flag

Ripples of color
waving against the sunrise
Old Glory stands proud

Bullets fly, blood runs,
my love, my life, is not just
a name on the wall

The fife, the drum, and
the mournful wail of bagpipes
tears heart from my chest

Stars and stripes folded
handed over by white gloves
will not warm my bed

Stepping Out on Faith

Tanka Prompt: Path

One step at a time

My heartbeat echoes my steps

Climbing higher yet.

Blindly I follow my path.

Fear be damned! I will succeed

Summer Breeze

Fear blossoms in my heart. Heat creeps up my spine. The devil's breath creeps closer.

Popping and crackling chases me from my home. I grab the things that mean the most to me — my fur-baby, photographs — my memories.

Damn that summer breeze whipping up the flames of the brush fires.

Tell Your Story

Seize inspiration
Whenever you find it near,
Grab hold with both hands

Don't hesitate now
Do not fear, grab it, mold it
To fit your vision

Experimental,
Traditional or combined
Make it share your voice

My Everything

I see him. Shiny bright curls brushing his collar. Soulful dark eyes hiding secrets. He is my world, my everything. The brass bell over the door jingles as he enters the café.

I pause, hidden in the shadows, waiting before I follow him through the double glass doors. Wouldn't want him to think I was stalking him, now would I? The scorched smell of burnt coffee tickles my nose.

Leaning against the counter, he laughs and flirts with my cousin, the barista. On the surface, he hasn't a care in the world.

Broad shoulders tapering to a narrow waist fill my sight. Heat flushes my cheeks. My heart speeds up. My pulse hammers in my ears.

I watch him take a seat in a leather armchair near the front windows. He sips his mocha grande, extra whipped cream, and opens his laptop.

I pay for my tall pike, black, slipping the barista a little extra and a wink. She smiles and slides a key beneath my napkins.

My cousin eats, sleeps, and breathes romance. Her world revolves around finding me a new soul mate. Can you have more than one?

Winding through waist-high chrome tables, I find a spot in the shadows in the far back corner of the cafe. I settle in with my back to the wall.

Good field of fire. Your words echo in my mind. Even when you are not with me, you are with me.

Memories assault me–the low rumble of your words, your touch, the heat of your breath against the back of my neck, your kiss. Enough! I can't think of you now. I need to focus on him.

I take a sip of my coffee. Bitter liquid scorches my tongue. Next time I will order a black tea. A caustic chuckle chokes me. Next time? There won't be a next time.

Surrounded by the clickety-clack of fingers flying across keyboards, I sit and wait. Time crawls by.

I watch a snail creeping across the floor. Inch by painful inch, it works its way to the door, to freedom. No one else sees the snail. There is a world beneath this one that no one sees. Just like you didn't see him. Just like he doesn't see me.

A patron heads for the exit, stepping on the snail on his way out. The snail's bid for freedom ends mere inches from the door. The crunch of the shattered shell matches the crunch of my shattered heart.

While my attention is on the snail and its ill-fated journey, night creeps in. Only he, I, and the barista remain.

It's time.

I gather my things, sticking my hand into my bag. A sharp prick reassures me it's still there. My fingers close around it. Standing, I nod to the barista.

She smiles, pointing at the key hook by the back door–reminding me to return the key when

I lock up and leave. Giving me a finger wave, she slips out. Silly girl, she thinks the world revolves around romance.

I walk to him, dropping into the chair next to him. This is the closest I have been to him in four years. His cologne washes over me. My breath hitches in my chest. My hands tremble. Darkness threatens the edges of my vision. My eyes close. Sucking in a deep breath, I center myself. My eyes open to see his bemused smile.

"Can I help you?" he asks.

I lean closer, invading his space. "You can die," I whisper.

He laughs. "Excuse me?" His eyebrows rise. "What did you say?" He looks around the café, slowly realizing everyone has left. Everyone except him and me, that is.

I move closer still, tilting my head to the side. I raise my voice, not a lot, just enough for him to hear me over the love song drifting in through the speakers. I speak slowly and clearly, enunciating each word. "I said you can die."

"Mike put you up to this, didn't he?" He looks around the café. "Where's the camera?"

"You don't recognize me, do you?" I pull the nine mm Sig Sauer from the holster beneath my shirttail. I lay the gleaming pistol in my lap.

It's smaller than the 1911s you used to carry, but it fits my hand.

His eyes land on the gun. Confusion crosses his face, but not fear, not yet. "Look, lady, I don't know who you are or what you want, but if this is some kind of prank, it's not funny."

Prank? Anger floods my system. I jerk my other hand from my purse. I fling the badge — your badge still splattered with your blood — against his chest.

The memories I fought to keep confined burst free. The horrified cries of 'officer down' on the radio, the knock on the door.

I remember my denial, my pain. Memories of the mad race through darkened streets lit by red and blue flashing lights, the scream of the siren matching the anguished cries torn from my chest threaten to overwhelm me.

"Prank?" I force the word between gritted teeth. "Was it a prank when you shot my husband in cold blood?" Spittle flies from my lips landing on his face.

My voice raises an octave, increases in volume. I move closer yet. "Was it a prank when you got off on a technicality?"

I grab the gun. I press the cold steel barrel against his forehead.

Images of you, bloody and pale, flood my mind. I feel the warmth slipping from your skin along with the life from your body. I hear your garbled goodbye.

Red rage encompasses my vision. I shove the barrel tighter against his head. I smell his fear.

"I'll show you prank." My fingers tighten on the trigger. I squeeze it gently like you taught me.

Nothing happens.

He scrambles backward, knocking over the armchair.

I look from the gun to him, back to the gun. Disappointment sweeps through me. How could I be so stupid? I forgot to chamber a round.

I rack the slide back and hear the round glide into place. My hands shake. The gun wavers in my grip.

He charges me. We fall to the floor, wrestling for control of the gun. Over and over we roll. Hands tugging, squeezing. Nails scratching, kicking, screaming. Your face crosses my mind. I relax.

The crack of the gunshot sounds muffled. Fire burns through my chest. Warm liquid gushes across my skin. I grow cold. My vision darkens.

I hear you calling.

"Hello, Darlin'," you say.

I reach for your outstretched hand and smile as you pull me from the darkness to your light.

Thank You

Thank you for taking the time to share my journey towards finding my voice. I hope you enjoyed it. As a reward for making it this far, I am going to share the unedited beginning of Broken Wings,the third novel in my Broken Badges series.

Broken Badges Series Blurb

Welcome to Bennett County, where the badge is heavy and the past never sleeps.

Here, the hot south Texas wind whispers secrets through the rusted skeletons of abandoned oil fields, and the past casts a long, twisted shadow.

Meet the men and women of Bennett County law enforcement: a fractured mosaic of Texas Rangers, investigators, highway patrol officers, and sheriff's deputies. Each officer carries their own scars—addiction, loss, secret identities, trauma. Their badge is a shield, but it can't protect what is already shattered.

When darkness descends on Bennett County, these broken badges become the only thing standing between the innocent and oblivion. Each case is a brutal puzzle, a fight against time, and a desperate search for redemption. As they face ruthless criminals, twisted minds, a damaged justice system, and their own inner demons, they must ask themselves: can they find absolution pursuing justice in a place as broken as they are, or will the darkness consume them first?

Broken Badges is a gritty, suspenseful series that explores the psychological toll of violence on those who fight it. It's for readers who crave hard-edged characters you can't help but root for, even as their flaws threaten to devour them, characters who stay with you long after the last page. Buckle up for a thrilling ride where justice is a battle hard-won, and the scars run deeper than the skin.

Broken Wings - Chapter One

Lexi stretched her arms over her head. Bending forward from the waist, she locked her fingers behind her head and twisted her shoulders from left to right. The tension from another twelve-hour shift slinging watered down drinks and dodging grabby hands released from her muscles. She straightened and rolled her head on her neck.

A cloud of blue-gray cigarette smoke dimmed the glow from the incandescent vintage firework bulbs dangling from the crown molding. Years of nicotine faded the once bright green of the Christmas tinsel wrapped around the lights to a dingy chartreuse.

A yawn cracked her jaw. She rubbed at her face as exhaustion tugged at her body. She crinkled her nose in disgust. The scent of stale beer and rotgut whisky soaked her fingers. Her shoulders sagged, her arms feeling as if they weighed a ton. Inhaling deeply, she popped her heavy eyelids open wide. She blew out a breath and shook her head. *Get a wiggle on.*

She dug her knuckles deep into her lower back trying to work out the ache of too many hours on too high stiletto heels. A groan escaped her lips to be swallowed by the mechanical bells and whistles of the slot machines. *I don't know how much longer I can do this.*

Pulling car keys from her tiny black crossbody bag, she cast a glance over at the burly bouncer sitting on a wooden bar stool near the casino's main exit. His biceps stretched the sleeves of his one-size-too-small uniform polo shirt as he crossed his powerful arms across his chest. The dim glow from the exit sign bounced a red glare off of his shaved, waxed head. She offered him a tired finger wave before opening the side door into the darkened alley. "Night, Robbie," she murmured, her words barely audible over the thumping bass of the house band banging out an off-key version of Twisted Sisters Heavy Metal Christmas.

The thick-necked bouncer raised his chin in her direction before turning his attention back to the dwindling crowd of drunks still tugging on the one-armed bandits. The metallic jingle of coins competed with the band.

Pausing in the doorway, she shivered in the frigid December air and tugged the hem of her sparkly micro-mini skirt down. If she hadn't been so tired and so dead set on avoiding Chad, the creepy night manager, she would've slipped into the staff locker room, showered, and changed into comfy yoga pants and a sweatshirt. Even the rancid cigarette smoke clinging to her hair couldn't motivate her to spend another moment in this building. *And I still have to study for tomorrow's pathophysiology exam.*

The flashing colored lights of the slot machines behind her cast flickering shadows in front of her. Rotting garbage overflowing the dumpster into the alley next to the door made her eyes water. She pinched her nostrils closed. It didn't help, so she dropped her hand. A skittering noise on the pavement chased a chill down her spine. She wove her keys between her fingers, sharp points facing outward. *Never be too cautious in this neighborhood. Wish the boss would let me carry a pistol. Or at least pepper spray.*

Lexi chuckled beneath her breath remembering the last time she'd brought pepper spray to work. She was lucky to still have a job and not be sitting behind bars at the Bennett county jail. If Chad had had his way, she'd be under the jail. *Jerk.* Thank goodness Robbie'd witnessed the entire event and wasn't afraid to stand up to the night manager.

The door slammed shut behind her, causing her to jump. Darkness swallowed the casino lights, the shouts of rowdy patrons, and the electronic bells ringing on the gaming machines. Silence enveloped her. Anemic strands of moonlight tried unsuccessfully to slither through the heavy cloud cover. She stood still, allowing her eyes to adjust to the darkness, wishing she had grabbed her jacket. A distant grumble of thunder added to her unease. A flash of lightning momentarily blinded her. She fumbled her cell phone from her bag and hit the flashlight button. No response.

Damn it. Dead again. She never remembered to charge her phone. Half the time she couldn't remember where she left it. She sighed. Feet aching in six-inch stilettos, she scanned the parking lot. *Another trudge through the darkness. Yay me.* At least this time, she'd snagged a parking space closer to the building than usual.

She took a step toward her jeep and a big, fat raindrop hit the tip of her nose and dripped off. The heavens opened up and rain poured down. *Great. Just freaking great.* She glared at the night sky. *You couldn't wait five lousy minutes?* She returned her attention to the parking lot. *Six more months. Six months until graduation and this job can kiss my—*

A rough cloth bag covered her face, obscuring her vision. Her phone and keys clattered to the ground. She struggled to breathe. Kicking and clawing, she fought until a sharp wasp-like sting smacked her on the back of the arm, sending a jolt of pain racing through her body. She couldn't move. Darkness wrapped around her like heavy draperies, holding her tight, suffocating her. Sheer panic flooded her system. Chills chased hot flashes down her chest. Waves of swirling nausea assaulted her.

"Quick, catch her before she falls. We need to get out of here."

Calloused hands jerked her from her feet as her limbs turned to jelly. Sinking beneath the influence of the drugs, she struggled to keep her eyes open, but felt herself floating away, the world around her fading into a distant haze.

**

Eyelids fluttering, Lexi swam to the surface of consciousness. Her mouth felt like it was stuffed with cotton. *Or dirty gym socks.* A hazy blur of shapes and colors surrounded her. Latex-covered fingers pressed on the inside of her wrist. An alcohol swab swept the bend of her elbow. The sharp prick of an IV needle sliding into her arm hurt for a moment before warmth rushed through her veins. A disorienting, floating sensation overwhelmed her.

Moans of a woman's pain mixed with an infant's shrill cry. *Where am I?*

The sound of her own labored breathing filled her ears. Just breathing took more energy than she could harness. With a heavy exhale, she slipped back into the welcoming darkness.

**

Strident beeping woke Lexi from her drugged sleep. Surrounded by deep voices, she struggled to understand their murmurs. Amidst the bass chorus, a soft soprano protested but was silenced by the sound of flesh hitting flesh. The metallic slide of a curtain being pulled across its rod competed with the muffled creaks of a patient trying to settle in a squeaky bed.

Lexi's nostrils flared. An overwhelming scent of disinfectant filled the air. She blinked her eyes rapidly, struggling to shake off her dazed state. *Must be in the ER again. When did I last eat?* She mentally berated herself. *Dummy. Doc warned you to watch your blood sugar.*

A blinding white light penetrated her closed eyelids. She winced and tried to raise an arm to shield her eyes but couldn't. A clanking metallic noise accompanied her aborted attempt. *What the…*

She tugged on her other arm. It wouldn't raise either. Cold steel bracelets surrounded her wrists. *Handcuffs?* She cracked her eyelids open, only to be met with the harsh glare of a spotlight. The intensity of the light painful, she squeezed her eyes closed.

Edging her fingers across the rough cotton covering her, she discovered she lay on a narrow, cot-like bed. Desperate to sit up, to move, to escape, she discovered a series of wide leather bands wrapped around her chest and waist, securing her in place.

She kicked out with her feet. Nothing. She was trapped. Her breath came faster. Adrenaline surged through her body. She thrashed against the restraints, struggling to free herself from the confines of the narrow hospital gurney. The room spun. Her stomach churned. Saliva gathered in the back of her mouth. Her heart raced, panic overtaking her. Heat flashed through her trembling muscles.

A sharp click echoed through the room, followed by the sound of heavy footsteps drawing closer. "Well, well, well, look who's awake?" A familiar whisky-soaked voice whispered in her ear. "We're not quite ready for you, sweetheart."

I know that voice. Who? With a surge of desperation, Lexi summoned every ounce of strength she possessed. She wrenched her wrists, feeling the metal bracelets bite into her flesh. Pain mingled with determination as she fought against her restraints. The clanking metallic noise grew louder as she struggled.

"Now, now, sweetie, fighting won't do any of us any good." A dark chuckle filled the air.

"Although I don't mind watching." A calloused hand patted her bare shoulder.

Bare shoulder? Where are my clothes? Her hands clenched and unclenched into fists. "Where…? Who…?" Her voice trembled. She tried to force words out of a throat that felt blocked, felt like she was choking. Tremors shook her body.

Sweat trickled down her forehead, mixing with the disinfectant's acrid scent. She strained against the leather bands, feeling the sting of her skin against the tight restraints.

A shadow fell across her face. She opened her eyes but all she could see was a dark silhouette wielding a hypodermic needle. A rush of icy-cold liquid filled her veins as she inserted the tip into the IV embedded in the crook of her elbow and pushed downward on the plunger. She gasped, her breath catching in her throat as her muscles spasmed involuntarily. She fought to cling to consciousness but was no match for the drugs. As they took hold once more, darkness tugged her back under.

Broken Wings - Chapter Two

As Sergeant Harper Evans lazily banked the
Airbus AS350 to the left, the vibrant lights of Redus
Creek shrank and faded into the distance. Through
the overhead skylight of the chopper, the inky night
sky unfolded like a vast expanse of black velvet
adorned with glimmering shards of shattered glass.
The muted hum of the rotor blades filled the cockpit
with a soothing whump-whump-whump. Sometimes
Harper felt as if her heart beat in time to the rhythm
of the rotors. A faint scent of aviation fuel mixed
with the plastic-y, chemical odor inherent to chopper
flight. *Peaceful. Boring, but peaceful.*

Beneath the helicopter, the south Texas
countryside grew increasingly dim, swallowed by the
encroaching night. A tiny sliver of the waxing moon
glistened just above the horizon. The flickering
flames of random flares, ignited to burn off excess
natural gas pockets from the vast expanse of oil wells

scattered across the brush country, danced in the distance. She scanned the gauges before her, carefully adjusting her flight helmet, feeling the weight of it on her head. A trickle of sweat made her scalp itch.

She couldn't help the weary sigh that escaped her lips, a mixture of exhaustion and frustration, a testament to the weariness that settled in after enduring a long, uneventful shift. Being a flight tactical officer for the Texas Department of Public Safety hadn't been her dream job, but returning home from the sandbox to find her younger sister, India, vanished destroyed a lot of her dreams. Broken dreams seemed to be a family tradition. While she'd grown to love her job over the past few months, she yearned for the day when she would command the aircraft from the coveted left-hand seat. Like she had in the Army.

Her co-pilot and DPS supervisor, Lieutenant Lincoln Sendero, glanced at his watch. A sly grin lifted the corners of his mouth exposing deep dimples. He stretched in his seat. Vertebrae popped audibly. "Have I told you how much I like a woman in uniform?" He reached over and fiddled with the zipper at the top of Harper's flight suit. "Especially you." He winked. "Out of uniform, too."

She slapped his hand away. "In your wildest dreams."

"Come on, Harper, you know we'd be great together. Just one drink. After shift." He tilted his head and deepened his grin.

Damn, I wish his dimples weren't so cute. Or his eyes so blue. If he wasn't such a douche, I could get lost in those eyes, like staring into the ocean on a stormy morning. She raised her pointer finger. "One, no. You're my supervisor. It's against the rules." She added her middle finger. "Two, no. We get off work at midnight. I have to go home to walk and feed Sheba and get to bed." Her ring finger joined the others. "And three, no. Just hell to the no."

"Sheba? Dogs can't tell time. She won't know if you're a little late." He wagged his eyebrows at her and dropped his voice to a husky Sam Elliott tone and added, "I can help you with the bed thing."

Harper scanned the flight gauges again. "Do you never give up?"

Lincoln shrugged. "Can't blame me for trying. One of these days you'll cave in." He looked at his watch again. "Two hours 'til shift change. Been a quiet night."

Her eyes narrowed into fierce slits, and her eyebrows furrowed in disbelief. The muscles in her jaw tightened, causing her cheeks to hollow slightly. She whipped her head in his direction and scowled. "You did not just use the Q word, did you?"

Lincoln laughed and tugged playfully on her ponytail. "Superstitious much?"

The radio mounted between their seats crackled to life. "Bennett County, DPS Charlie Tango 109. Officers requesting assistance."

"Quiet," Harper muttered. She glared at Lincoln. "You just had to say quiet, didn't you?" She keyed her mic. "DPS 109, go ahead County."

"We have deputies searching a brushy area three klicks northwest of the intersection of Old Kyote and Sand Branch roads. Suspect is an escaped convict from Atascosa County jail. Known to be armed and dangerous."

"10-4, County. We're five mikes out. En route." She pushed the cyclic forward to speed up and raised the collective to keep the chopper level.

"Charlie Tango 109, be advised, subject is said to have long rifles hidden in the brush."

"Acknowledged." *I hope they can last five minutes.* She increased the chopper's speed.

The radio crackled again. Static burst from the speakers, followed by the popping sounds of rapid gunfire. A frantic voice called out. "Shots fired. Shots fired."

As the rush of adrenaline coursed through Harper's veins, her sense heightened. Every beat of her racing heart echoed in her ears, competing with the pounding of the chopper blades. The world around her seemed to move in slow motion, each passing second stretching into an eternity.

Harper's mouth felt parched, as if all moisture had been sucked out of it. She swallowed hard, desperately trying to moisten her dry throat. Time seemed to stretch. To almost stand still.

With each passing second, the chopper sliced through the air with increased velocity. Harper tightened her grip on the control stick. Her muscles trembled with the strain of pushing it forward. She could feel the vibrations of the aircraft beneath her, responding to her every command, adding to her sense of urgency.

Every muscle in her body tensed, her grip on the control stick becoming almost painful. The familiar vibrations of the helicopter's engine resonated through her fingertips, grounding her in the present moment but the echoes of the past were too strong to ignore.

Her fear for the officers on the ground combined with the adrenaline racing through her veins transported her back to the war zone. In her mind, the brush country faded, giving way to a vivid memory of the endless scorching red desert sands of a foreign country. She squeezed her eyes closed, feeling the gritty texture of airborne sand invading her uniform. The weight of her memories bore down on her, threatening to suffocate her in their relentless grip.

***

The pungent smell of gunpowder lingered in the air, intermingled with the acrid scent of burning oil wells and the metallic odor of blood. Images of tracer fire emblazoned the backside of her eyelids. Her breath grew ragged. Every nerve in her body trembled on edge. Deafening explosions echoed in her ears, accompanied by the haunting screams of her fallen comrades. Her knuckles whitened as she clutched the stick.

The helicopter jolted violently, shaking her to the core. The blades whirred above her head, cutting through the air like a scythe. Through the windshield, she could see the chaos unfolding below. Smoke billowed from crumbling buildings, fires dotted the desert and devoured a once vibrant city. The bedlam of war unfolded around her.

With a surge of raw power, she maneuvered the helicopter through the storm of violence. Dodging bullets and evading missiles, the desert sands blurred beneath her. The wind howled in her ears. Explosions blossomed, sending shockwaves through the air. A convoy of enemy vehicles—ragged pickup trucks, jeeps, and tanks—raced across the dunes, leaving a wake of destruction in its wake.

She dove low, skimming the unforgiving terrain. The desert sands whipped up, creating a blinding sandstorm. She pushed the chopper to its *limits. Her hands, soaked with sweat, danced across*

the control panel unleashing a barrage of firepower.

The deafening roar of the guns drowned out all else.

Through the haze and smoke, she glimpsed

the twisted wreckage of vehicles, their metal

carcasses smoldering beneath the chopper. The

searing heat from the explosions radiated through the

air, leaving a blistering sensation on her exposed

arms.

A hailstorm of bullets punctuated the air with

sharp cracks, tearing through the metal hull of the

chopper. A missile shrieked. Harper banked sharply

away from the projectile. Sweat soaked her clothing,

making it cling to her like a second skin.

Every fiber of her being screamed for safety,

yet she clung tightly to the helicopter controls,

navigation across the war-torn landscape.

"We're hit. We're hit." Panic filled her co-pilot's voice.

Beep-beep-beep. *The stall warning horn blared. The light flashed on the dash. A voice screamed in her headset. "Brace, brace, brace. We're going down."*

***

"Harper? Harper?" Lincoln snapped his fingers in front of her face. Placing a hand on her shoulder, he gave her a sharp shake. "Evans!"

Jarred, she returned to the present. As her mind replayed the haunting scenes of war, the physical effects of her emotions manifested. Beads of sweat formed on her forehead, trickled down her temples. The tightness in her chest intensified, constricting her breath and causing her heart to race erratically. Her lungs struggled to draw in enough air. The taste of sand filled her mouth as if she were back in that foreign desert, the dryness of the air parching her throat. Her hand shook as she reached for a bottle of water. She scanned the gauges again.

Harper fought to regain control of herself, to separate the past from the present. With every ounce of strength she possessed, she forced her grip on the control stick to relax. Her knuckles regained their color as the tension ebbed away. She took a deep breath, filling her lungs with the crisp air of the present moment. The memories, horrible memories, still lingered but she refused to let them control her.

She was a warrior, a survivor who had faced the horrors of war. She exhaled, her body trembling with exhaustion. The scars of battle would forever mark her. She would always battle the demons within. *And I will win.*

She pushed the stick forward, urging the helicopter to fly faster, to get to the officers needing their help.

"Where'd you go?"

"Nowhere." Harper made eye contact with her partner. "I'm here. I'm good."

Lincoln studied her face. "No, you're not. Take a breath. I've got the stick." He took control of the helicopter. "Did you ever visit Dr. Wallace?"

Harper leaned back in her seat. Shook the tension from her hands. "I don't need a shrink."

Harper's thoughts turned to the officers on the ground. Her fingers itched with the need to regain control of the chopper. *Four mikes.* She imagined their faces, their voices pleading for help. Every passing second felt like a weight upon her chest, urging her to go faster, to reach their destination in record time. She leaned forward in her seat as if doing so would help the aircraft move faster. The weight of those officers' lives rested on her shoulders.

The minutes ticked away, and with every passing moment, the intensity of her emotions grew. Fear mingled with hope, creating a potent cocktail of emotions that fueled her every move. As more cries for help issued from the radio, she thought, *I hope they can last four minutes.*

***

Harper rolled her head on her shoulders, stretching her neck to relieve tension. It didn't work. She shoehorned her flight suit into the cramped metal confines of her locker, the fire-resistant Nomex fabric rustling against itself. She swiftly swapped her olive-green flight helmet for a sleek black motorcycle one, the cool touch of the smooth surface soothing beneath her fingertips. Slinging her bag over one shoulder, she slammed the heavy locker door shut,

169

the loud clang echoing through the squad room. She spun the lock with fingertips.

With purposeful strides, the sturdy heels of her motorcycle boots resounded with a satisfying clump on the freshly polished tile floor of the law enforcement center's lobby. As she made her way towards the exit, the faint scent of cleaning agents wafted through the air, mingling with the faint smell of gasoline and burned popcorn. With a nod and smile that fell far short of happiness, Harper raised her hand in a farewell wave to the dispatchers, their figures barely visible behind the darkly tinted bulletproof glass enclosing the communications center.

She shoved open the double glass doors of the Bennett County Law Enforcement Center and stepped outside four hours past her normal shift change. Even this late at night, heat and humidity sucked the breath from her lungs. In the dark, she stumbled over a pothole in the parking lot. Exhaustion swamped her. She paused for a moment, reflecting on her shift.

A heavy knot formed in her stomach, twisting and churning. Her muscles ached with tension. She could feel the tightness in her chest, a physical manifestation of the emotional burden she carried.

The air around her felt suffocating. Barely June and the temperatures were already breaking triple digits. Hurricanes were forming in the Atlantic. The stormy weather mirrored her mental status. First she lost control of herself. Fell victim to her memories and then… she shook her head. She couldn't think about that right now.

The humidity clung to her skin, making it clammy and damp, amplifying the discomfort consuming her. Each breath she took was shallow and labored. Beads of sweat trickled down her temples, mingling with the tears that welled up in her eyes. *Damn it!* She wasn't going to be able to put off thinking about tonight's shift after all.

Taking potshots at a DPS helicopter was never a good idea. She could still hear the report of the rifles. Feel the kick of the butt against her shoulder leaving behind a bruise.

She closed her eyes and said a quick prayer for the soul of the escaped convict. She scrubbed a hand across her face. Rubbed her chest, her touch almost desperate, as if trying to physically erase the weight that lay heavy upon her breast. She didn't know for sure that her shot ended the young man's life. Unlike some of the testosterone-filled braggarts claiming the kill shot, she didn't want to know. Taking a life never sat easily on her shoulders. She hoped it never did.

She reopened her eyes and gazed up at the night sky, searching for solace. The stars blinked back at her, their distant glow offering a glimmer of reassurance. She closed her eyes once more, her lips again moving silently in prayer. She sought forgiveness for the life she may have been forced to take.

But even as she whispered her prayers, a lingering unease remained. The memory of the shots fired at the DPS helicopter replayed in her mind, followed by her answering fire. EAch gunshot echoed like a haunting refrain, a constant reminder of the irreversible consequences of her actions. No matter how hard she tried, she couldn't shake off the guilt.

Across the parking lot, Lincoln raised a hand in farewell. "Enjoy your time off," he yelled before climbing into his lifted pickup truck.

"You, too," she replied. *Administrative leave.*

Yippee. More time to spend dodging Jess's calls.

Please note the sarcasm. At least the investigation

shouldn't take too long. It was a good shoot. If there

is such a thing. She hoped Ranger Trammell or

Ranger Morgan caught the case. They knew her.

Trusted her morality and judgment. *I had no choice.*

Her shoulders slumped. *Yeah, just keep telling*

yourself that, sunshine. Maybe someday you'll even

believe it. Her chin dropped to her chest. *Ah, crap.*

Jess. I'm going to have to tell her about the shooting

before she reads about it on social media. I hate

social media. Why can't people just mind their own

business?

Jessica, Harper's older sister, had shouldered

the job of raising Harper and India when their parents

died in a fiery car crash. One minute her parents were

there, nagging her about curfews and hanging out

with the wrong people, and Jess was in college. The next, they were gone, and Jess's dreams of medical school had gone up in smoke with them. *More broken dreams.*

Harper unlocked the saddlebags on her Harley Street Glide and tossed her flight bag inside. Jess hated her riding a bike. Said it was too dangerous. Hated Harper's job for the same reason. *Probably why I do both.*

As she swung her leg over the bike, she heard sobbing coming from behind her. *Ignore it. None of your business. It's been a long, long night. Just go home.*

She fired up the bike's engine. It rumbled to life with a beefy growl. The vibrations tickled her thighs. A deep breath escaped her chest. *Damn it.* Jerking the key from the switch, she clambered off the bike.

A young woman huddled in the shadows beneath the ancient oak tree at the edge of the parking lot. Arms wrapped around her knees, her head rested on her forearms. Her shoulders shook with sobs.

An image of her younger sister flashed through her mind. *Could it be? After all this time? Finally?* "Indy?" Harper called out to the young woman as she rushed toward her. "India, is that you? Where have you been? We've been worried sick."

The woman started. She glanced around the parking lot, and spotting Harper, jumped to her feet and took off running. She stumbled and almost fell. Finding her balance, she continued to run.

"What the…?" Ignoring her fatigue, Harper sprinted after the girl. "Hey, wait," she called out, urgency raising the pitch of her voice.

The woman hesitated, stopped running. She turned to face Harper. Took a hesitant step in her direction.

In the glow of a street lamp, Harper could see tears glistening on the girl's cheeks. Saw her pregnant belly. Other than the swollen abdomen, the girl looked starved. Like she had been living on the street for a long time.

Limp, unwashed dark hair fell into her eyes. She looked to be barely out of college. Disappointment crushed Harper's heart as she realized she didn't recognize the young woman. The tactical flight officer stepped toward her, approaching slowly. As she got closer, she noticed the tattered condition of her ill-fitting clothing. As if they belonged to someone else. She held out a hand and gentled her voice. "You okay? I'm a police officer. Can I help you? Is there someone I can call for you?"

At the word police, fear flashed in the young woman's eyes. She backed away, spun on her heels and rabbited away.

Harper's feet pounded against the pavement as she chased the woman through the dimly lit streets. Questions flooded her mind. *Who is this woman? Why is she running from me? Why is she afraid of the police?* She willed her legs to move faster as the girl pulled away from her. She was deceptively fast for her condition. *Don't lose her.*

Her tight chest labored to expand. She wheezed as she struggled to pull in a full breath. She exhaled noisily. *Too much sitting.* She gasped for air. Despite the exhaustion weighing on her, Harper lengthened her stride and pumped her arms, fueled by her innate sense of duty and the urgency of the situation. This young woman cannot disappear into the night. *I won't lose another one.*

Up ahead, the young girl darted around a sharp corner. Her footsteps echoed against the brick-walled building lining the street. Harper kicked harder, pushing off the uneven concrete and wishing she'd worn running shoes instead of biker boots. Turning the corner, she skidded to a stop, her boots screeching against the ground and leaving faint black rubber skid marks on the sidewalk.

The deserted street stretched out before her, devoid of any signs of life. Slowly, she turned her head left and right, her eyes frantically searching for any trace of the elusive girl. The silence was deafening, broken only by the distant hum of traffic and the chirping of crickets. The scent of asphalt and exhaust lingered in the air, mingling with the faint odor of freshly cut grass from a vacant lot sporting a giant for sale sign. Confusion etched lines on her forehead as she furrowed her eyebrows, trying to make sense of the situation. She scanned her surroundings again paying special attention to the shadows. A hot breeze crawled across the hairs on her arms. Goosebumps formed on her skin as she shivered, a premonition washing over her. *I feel death.*

Spinning, she searched the street behind her. Still no sign of the young woman. Moving slower, Harper continued down the road, peering into alleyways and door stoops. Up ahead, a large office building loomed. She picked up her pace. Reaching the building, she pulled on the front door. Locked. She rattled it. Pressed her face against the polished glass and peered into the dimly lit lobby.

Frustration and disappointment pushed down on her shoulders. *Where could she have gone?* She spun in a slow circle. Her eyes scanned her surroundings again. Her fingers tapped restlessly against her thighs as she tried to catch her breath. She replayed the chase in her mind. With a shake of her head, she sent one last glance up and down the street. Accepting defeat, she shrugged and turned to trek back to her motorcycle.

As Harper rounded the corner, the sharp sound of glass shattering reverberated through the air. She swiftly pivoted, her gaze catching sight of a young woman suspended perilously from the second floor of the office building she had attempted to access; the building with the locked door.

Harper gasped, her eyes widening in shock. Time froze as she watched the young woman's body hurtle towards the unforgiving ground. A horrifyingly, wet thump echoed through the air, sending shivers down Harper's spine.

Harper screamed and collapsed onto the ground, curling into a ball. Shaking, she rocked back and forth, hands pressed against her ears. A keening whisper escaped her, the sound a cross between a muffled scream and a whimper. She swallowed hard, forcing bile back down her throat. *I will never forget that sound as long as I live.* Time stopped as she was swept into the past for the second time that evening.

*****

Hot air swept through the cockpit of the helicopter. The whooshing whine of a rocket-propelled grenade induced a flash of pure terror. She shoved the stick forward, hard, pushing the chopper into a fast, steep dive to avoid being hit. PUlling up sharply, she banked right as a second grenade was launched at them. The rat-a-tat-tat of automatic rifle fire followed the grenade. A hair-raising scream sounded from the open door behind her. She looked back just in time to see her intelligence officer plummet to the ground.

*****

Fighting her way back to the present, not knowing how much time she'd lost, she dug into her jeans pocket. Hands shaking, she pulled out her cell phone and dialed 9-1-1 as she ran back down the sidewalk, knowing there was no aid to be offered. The phone rang in her ear.

"9-1-1-, what is your emergency?"

"Elaine? This is Sergeant Evans, DPS Charlie Tango 109. I'm in the 500 block of Anderson Road." Harper took a deep breath to still the shakiness in her voice. "I need EMS, the on-call officer, and most likely the on-call JP on-scene. A young woman just fell—or jumped—from the second story of the Manske building here." She approached the front of the building. She scrambled over the wooden privacy fence surrounding the property. "I'll check vitals and—what the hell?"

"Sergeant Evans? Are you code four?"

Harper felt a sudden jolt as her phone slipped from her grasp and hit the ground with a resounding thud. Startled, she quickly stepped back, her heart pounding in her chest. She looked up. *Yes, there's the broken window. What the ever-loving hell?*

Confusion and disbelief washed over her. Scanning her surroundings, she searched frantically for any sign of the girl she had seen moments ago. Nothing. No body, no girl, no trace of… anything. Just a mocking emptiness.

Sirens wailed in the distance, their piercing sound growing louder with each passing moment. Intermittent flashes of red and blue lights shattered the darkness, casting an eerie glow on the surroundings. With a trembling hand, she scooped her phone from the ground, feeling the coolness of the device against her palm. Speaking calmly into the receiver, she assured the concerned dispatcher she was safe and unharmed. *Physically, anyway.* "The first officers are arriving on scene. Thank you, Elaine."

Harper noticed a rushing noise. Turning on her flashlight, she examined the scene around her. A faucet on the side of the building ran full blast, flooding the sidewalk, leaving puddles everywhere. If evidence of a body hitting the ground had existed, it was long gone.

She buried her face in her hands. Guilt pushed down on her shoulders. *How much time did I lose? How could I have freaked out like that?* She sobbed into her hands as the events of the night caught up with her. Despair wrapped around her like a cloak smothering her ability to think rationally. *How can I save India when I can't even find a young woman who was standing right in front of me?*

As the first patrol unit slid to a stop and shut off its blaring siren, Harper dashed the tears from her face. She stiffened her spine and pulled herself back together—at least superficially. It went against her very being to exhibit signs of vulnerability. Stiff upper lip and all that jazz. A dark chuckle escaped. *Might be why I'm still single.*

Deputy Annabelle Lee, the only female deputy in the department, emerged from her patrol unit, the door closing behind her with a solid thud that echoed in the quiet street. Adjusting her duty belt, she tugged her uniform pants up and pulled her straw Bangora hat down on her forehead. She wiped sweat from her face with the back of her hand.

Annabelle hated her name, hated being teased all throughout school about the poem that claimed love transcended death. She demanded to be addressed by her last name only. Her strong personality and black belt in jiu-jitsu ensured everyone complied. Harper enjoyed working with her.

"Got here as fast as we could." Lee held out a slender, well manicured hand in greeting. Clasping Harper's hand firmly, she shook it and asked, "So, Evans, whatcha' got going?"

Lee's trainee, Deputy Edson Garner, climbed out of the opposite side of the vehicle. As he approached, a warm breeze swept down the street bringing with it the scents of hot pavement, automobile exhaust, and his cologne, a strong combination of cedar and leather. Harper thought she detected a tiny whiff of the copper penny smell often associated with blood, but with all the competing scents, she couldn't be sure.

Garner removed his hat and flipped his sun-kissed wheat blond hair from his shirt collar. He rubbed the back of his neck with his long, masculine fingers digging into the knotted muscles beneath his skin. He blew out a sharp breath and glanced at Harper. "Remind me to never let her drive again."

Harper scoffed. "As if you really have a choice." She stepped away from the puddle of water pooling on the cracked sidewalk, careful not to track through it. *Not that any evidence can be pulled from it.*

The smell of dampness, partially from the heavy humidity and partially from the running faucet, hung in the oppressive night air. Along the horizon, heat lightning sizzled and flashed from cloud to cloud, lighting up their bruised purple underbellies and bringing with it the pungent bleach-like smell of ozone.

She turned off her flashlight, its beam fading into darkness, and turned to face the deputies. "I'm not sure." She felt her forehead crinkle as confusion filled her mind. She bit her lip. "I know I heard her fall," Harper said, her husky voice laced with uncertainty. Her tongue darted out to moisten her lips. She summoned a deep breath. Held it for a long moment before releasing it forcefully. She pointed to the ground beneath the shattered window where glimmers of broken glass reflected the patrol vehicle's headlights. "Right here. She fell right here."

Lee and Garner exchanged a look, their eyes filled with a measure of disbelief. They watched Harper closely, concern etched on their faces. Lee's eyebrows drew together as she rubbed the skin on her throat, pinching at it.

"Talking about me again at the office, are they?" Harper's shoulders folded inward. Her arms wrapped around in her middle in a self-hug. "Don't believe everything you hear. I'm not crazy."

"Hey, now," Lee interrupted. "No one said you were crazy."

Garner shoved his hands deep into his polyester uniform pants pockets and avoided making eye contact. He cleared his throat and rocked back on his heels. Tipping his head to the side, he studied the ground beneath the window. As his eyes narrowed, his analytical mind appeared to race, his thoughts dancing across his face as it looked like he was trying to piece together a tricky puzzle.

Red and blue lights flooded the scene as the ambulance, followed by two more unmarked vehicles, slid to a stop. Paramedics carrying a jump bag and a backboard jumped from the ambulance. Plainclothes sheriff's department investigators stepped out of the matching unmarked Ford F150s. More marked patrol units descended on their location.

Must be a slow night. Or maybe the peacocks are just looking for a new photo op. Harper shook the tension out of her hands. Other than Lee, the token female deputy on the force, she didn't think very highly of the sheriff's department. Ever since Sheriff Preston's health forced him into an early retirement and Judge Scott pushed the Commissioner's Court to appoint Blake Wezzle as interim Sheriff, all the outstanding officers she had trusted, that she worked well with, had either quit or been forced out of the department.

"I heard about your sister. I'm so sorry. Any luck yet?" Lee asked. Empathy softened her words. "I also heard that you had a rough shift. Killing a man is never easy, even when it's deserved."

Harper's eyes widened, a flicker of frustration passing through them. "I'm not crazy. I know what I saw," she insisted. "Young girl, early twenties, dark hair and a swollen belly. Probably six months pregnant. I chased her from the LEC to this spot, and then she vanished. I turned to leave and heard glass shatter. Saw her dangling out the window. For God's sake, I heard her body hit the ground. There is no way she could have run away."

Garner shrugged, his shoulders rising and falling with uncertainty. "No one is saying you're crazy," he replied. "But if someone fell from that window, they didn't get up and walk away." He gestured to the empty surroundings. "So, where is she?"

Paramedic Ramos dropped the jump bag on the ground at his feet. He repeated Garner's question. "Where's our patient?"

Harper felt a knot tightening in her stomach as frustration mixed with anxiety. A shadow flitted across her face. Her hands trembled ever so slightly, betraying the intensity of her emotions. "I don't know." She bit the words out.

Taking a deep breath, she tried to steady her emotions. The scene before her seemed to mock her, broken glass providing evidence of a fall, but no trace of the girl who had supposedly fallen. It was as if the ground had swallowed her whole, erasing any proof she had ever existed at all.

Suddenly, a rustling noise came from a dark corner behind the privacy fence. Harper's heart skipped a beat as she switched her flashlight back on. With a sharp gesture, she indicated to the others that they should stay back. Flashlight gripped tightly in her clammy hands, she crept toward the noise, careful not to startle whoever might be hiding in the shadows. Sweat trickled down her spine, pooling at the waistband of her pants.

The beam of her light sliced through the darkness illuminating a stack of abandoned appliance boxes. Senses on high alert, she knelt in front of the stack. She reached a hand forward to move the top box. Just as she touched it, a gray brindle cat screeched and shot out from beneath it. Startled, Harper flinched backwards and lost her balance. The flashlight shot from her hands, the bulb shattering upon impact. She fell flat on her tailbone, cracking it against the pavement.

Lee hustled to her side and held out a hand to help her up.

Harper ignored her hand. "Look." She pointed down the sidewalk. A tiny trail of blood spatter led away from where they were. She rushed to her feet, and limping, she followed the trail until it vanished—just like the young girl. "What the hell?" Uncertainty colored her voice. She looked at Lee.

"You saw that, right? I'm not imagining a blood trail, am I?"

Lee and Garner exchanged another glance, their expressions mirroring Harper's confusion. The weight of the mystery hung heavy in the air, and the silence was deafening, broken only by the sound of rushing water from the faucet.

"Why don't you have a seat over here while we look around?" Lee asked, pointing to the edge of the sidewalk. "Try to find a dry spot. I'm going to look around a bit, and I'll be back with you."

Harper plopped gingerly on the curb, the rough texture of the concrete pushing through her blue jeans. She pulled at a torn cuticle and waited. As she sat there, cooling her heels, she overheard snippets of conversation between the paramedics and the investigators. They spoke of missing girls and unsolved cases. She watched as people emerged from their homes drawn by the morbid curiosity that always accompanied a crime scene. *If it is a crime scene.*

Harper's mind raced, trying to piece together the events that had just unfolded. She replayed the sound of the glass shattering in her mind, the image of the young woman dangling in the air and crashing to the ground. *Why didn't she cry out?*

As the seconds ticked by, the reality of the situation sank in. Harper's brow furrowed further. *How long was I out of it? How long was I lost in the past?* Standing, she approached the group of gossiping first responders. "What's this about missing girls?"

A chilling silence met her as they all stopped talking. One of the investigators she know in passing looked around the group before turning his attention to Harper. "I don't know what you are talking about."

Slipping on latex gloves, Lee walked over and turned off the spigot, stopping the water pooling on the sidewalk before it could wash away any more evidence. She approached Harper.

"Damn," Harper said. "I should have already shut that off." A pleading tone entered her voice. "Lee, I don't know how many times I have to say it. I promise I am not crazy. I don't know what's going on here, but I'm not crazy."

"Look, Evans, I don't know what's going on here either, but I know you. You're as solid as they come. If you said something happened, I believe you. We just need to figure it out."

Garner's voice filled with a mixture of skepticism and curiosity as he asked, "But where do we even begin? It's like she vanished into thin air." He tossed a distrustful look toward Harper before turning back to his partner. "If she even existed in the first place."

Harper growled at Garner. "She existed."

Garner held his hands in front of himself, palms facing toward Harper. "Hey, I'm just looking at the evidence—or lack of it. I'm not saying it didn't happen. I'm just saying I see nothing here to back up your story."

Lee faced her trainee and said, "Let's get some help out here and canvas the neighborhood. Chances are slim to none that anyone saw anything at this time of night, but we have to do something."

Harper's gaze shifted from the doubting deputy to the broken window to the surrounding area. She grabbed her left elbow with her right hand. Her left thumbnail unconsciously went into her mouth. She chewed the nail while she scanned the scene, searching for any overlooked detail, any sign that could shed light on the mysterious disappearance.

The flickering street lights cast long shadows, adding an eerie ambience to the already perplexing situation. Realizing she was biting her nails, she jerked her hand from her mouth.

Harper stiffened her spine. Put her shoulders back and stood taller. She continued studying the area. "There." She pointed to a security camera mounted above the double doors of the building. Spinning around, she spotted several more security cameras in the area. "We need that footage. All of it." She glared at Garner. "And it's not a story. It happened."

Garner nodded. "I'll gather the surveillance footage from this and the nearby buildings. If someone fell from that window, there should be some evidence to support it."

"I'm going to retrace my steps," Harper said, her voice firm with resolve. "I must have missed something, something that will identify the girl or help me find her. Something to make sense of this."

Tires screeched as a fancy SUV skidded to a stop, bouncing over a curb. The engine's growl silenced as the smell of burned gasoline filled the air. Sheriff Blake Wezzle stepped from the driver's side of the vehicle and sauntered over to where the trio gathered. County Judge Jan Scott fell into step behind him.

Seeing them standing side by side was like seeing Jack Spratt and his wife from the nursery rhyme. Wezzle stood 6'4" tall and looked like he never ate. A long horse face, thin chest, and limbs like twigs, he looked like a stiff breeze could blow him away.

Judge Scott, on the other hand, was, to use a severe understatement, solidly built. Standing not quite 5'4", she weighed in at close to 290 pounds. A walking heart attack waiting to happen, she was overly fond of wearing all white. Tonight's suit comprised a blazer, vest, pencil skirt and Dakota stitched leather cowboy boots. She topped off the look with a white Stetson.

I wonder where her cigar is? Harper dragged her hands down her face, wiping away the disbelief. *Who in their right mind wears white to a crime scene?* Harper disliked the sheriff and judge equally. They reminded her of an old television sitcom from the early 1980s with a couple of good old boys, a crooked sheriff, and a corrupt judge. *Hey, if the shoe fits...* She didn't trust either one of them as far as she could throw them.

"Deputies, what's going on here?" growled Sheriff Wezzle.

"Sheriff," Harper began.

He held up a hand cutting her off. "Evans, why are you here? You're on administrative leave pending an officer involved shooting investigation. Go home."

"But, Sheriff, she's a witness."

"Witness to what?" Disgust laced his voice. "A water faucet left on overnight? Drop it, Lee." He looked around the ground, glanced down the sidewalk. "Nothing happened here. Why are we wasting my resources? Lee, you have calls holding. Get back to work while you still have a job, before you find yourself suspended." He threw another look at Harper. "Unlike DPS, we don't suspend people with pay."

Intimidated, Garner ducked his head and speed walked back to their patrol vehicle. Lee cast an apologetic look at Evans before doing the same.

"Sheriff, you need to check that security footage. Canvas the neighborhood. Do something. There's a wounded, pregnant girl out here somewhere. She needs our help."

"Evans," snapped the sheriff, "I know you don't work for me. Lord knows I never would have hired you. Do I need to call your supervisor? Get out of here. Now."

As she walked away, Harper heard the sheriff walk over to his throng of sycophantic deputies and investigators. Disgust laced his gravelly voice. "Crazy woman. She probably made the whole thing up. Freakin' hysterical females. Never been the same since she came back from overseas. That's why women shouldn't be allowed in combat. I'll never understand why women want to act like men in the first place. Hell, I bet her sister's not really missing. I bet she just took off somewhere to get away from all the crazy in her family."

Harper whirled on her heel and stormed back to the sheriff. Heat burned her cheeks. She forced her way through the crowd of laughing yes men and shoved a finger in his chest. Punctuating each word with a new jab, she spat the words at him through clenched teeth. "I am not hysterical. I do not make things up. I know what I say, you pompous ass. And as far as my sister…"

Sheriff Wezzle puffed up. His face turned brilliant red. "Why you little…" he sputtered. His hands tightened into fists.

Before he could say or do anything else, Judge Scott intervened. "Sheriff," she said in a warning tone. She tapped a toe against the pavement. "Both of you need to step back, calm down, and let the investigators do their jobs."

The sheriff narrowed his eyes. Stepped closer to Harper.

The judge stepped between them and laid a hand against his chest. "Sheriff."

He shrugged off her touch and turned away. He muttered beneath his breath as he walked away. "No job to be done. Just another useless cunt lying for attention."

"Sheriff! Go. Now." Judge Scott pointed at the SUV waiting on the curb. "I mean it. Leave. Immediately."

He started to retort but huffed out a breath instead. "Fine," he snapped before stalking over to the waiting vehicle. Climbing into the driver's seat, he slammed the door, fired up the engine and peeled away, tires spinning and kicking up loose gravel.

Judge Scott sighed. Ran a hand through her hair. "Sorry about that, Evans." Moving closer to

Harper, she tilted her head up to meet her eyes. She placed a pudgy, bejeweled hand on her arm. Patted it supportively. "I'm sorry about the sheriff's behavior. He's under a lot of pressure." She sighed. "Looks like I'm going to have to catch a ride home with one of the investigators. Before I go, can I give you a bit of advice?"

Harper shrugged. "Sure, I guess."

"Go home. Get some rest. You've been through a hell of a night. I don't need to remind you that the sheriff and your boss are poker buddies, do I?" She raised one platinum eyebrow and dropped her hands onto her paunchy hips. "It's a man's world. Ladies need to stick together. Seriously, go home."

"Fine." Harper trudged back to the parking lot where her bike waited. She wove her hair into a loose braid and tied it off with the hair tie wrapped around her wrist. She pulled on her helmet and slung a leg over the motorcycle. As she did, a flash of indignation mixed with rage flooded her system. "Fuck the sheriff's department and fuck that boss hogg bitch judge. I know what I saw. They'll see. I'm going to find that girl."

For comments or more information, please email me at:

glenda@rattlerpress.com

Or check out my website:

rattlerpress.com

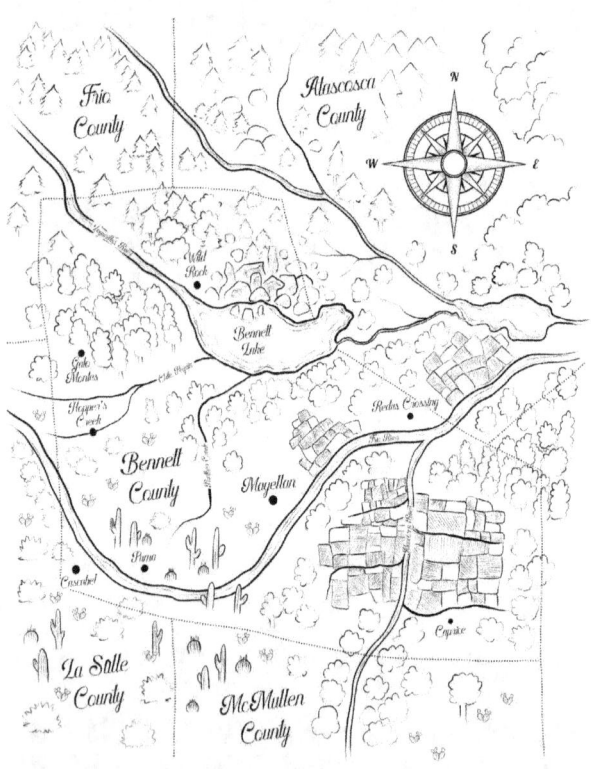